The boulder Brendon had been trying to remove was oval shaped, about two feet long and a foot across. Most of it was gray-brown and mottled, perfectly camouflaged by the surrounding dirt.

However, Brendon had struck one edge of the stone with enough force to chip off the outer layer of rock.

The gash wasn't white or gray, or even the orangeish red of the iron-ore rocks he sometimes found.

No, under the dirt and the first layer of stone was a pretty, pale blue layer...a blue-dragon-egg rock.

# Of Myst and Folly

**Leah Cutter**

Book View Café
www.BookViewCafe.com

# Also by Leah Cutter

**Historic Fantasy:**
*Paper Mage*
*The Caves of Buda*
*The Jaguar and the Wolf*
*A Sword's Poem*

**Contemporary Fantasy:**
*Poisoned Pearls*
*The Popcorn Thief*
*Siren's Call*
*When the Moon Over Kualina Mountain Comes*
*Zydeco Queen and the Creole Fairy Courts*

**The Shadow Wars Trilogy:**
*The Raven and the Dancing Tiger*
*The Guardian Hound*

**The Clockwork Fairy Kingdom Trilogy:**
*The Clockwork Fairy Kingdom*
*The Maker, the Teacher, and the Monster*

**Collections:**
*Beyond the Garden*
*Burning Flowers*
*Tell Me Again*
*The Shadow Wars*
*The Shredded Veil Mysteries*

# Of Myst and Folly

**Leah Cutter**

# Prologue

## I

**U**gh," Brendon complained as his shovel hit, *hard,* against yet another rock. His arms jolted back from the force and a clear tinging sound rang across the open soccer field. The summer sun still hung low in the morning sky, casting long shadows from the trees around the edges of the cleared area. Soon, it would rise high enough to be blinding, and Brandon would be sweating up a storm. For now, it was one less thing to add to his long, *long* list of complaints.

Starting with the dead city of Seattle to the north, just beyond the trees and hills, shadowed by sun and *myst.*

"Dad, I swear, this field is all rocks with just a little bit of dirt holding them together," Brendon grumbled as he put his shovel down and reached for the seven-foot-long iron digging bar. He probed the edges of the stone. It was another huge one. At least the grass was all dead, making the rocks easier to see.

Hopefully they'd be able to protect this field better from the *myst.* It sucked that their other field had been spoiled. Particularly this late in the season.

With a deep breath, Brendon raised the bar over his head and heaved. The end sank deep into the soft earth. A small flush of satisfaction ran through Brendon. He was stronger now than he had been when he'd started working with Dad in the field just a few weeks before, on his fourteenth birthday. Able to lift the bar higher, send it into the ground with more force.

As Brendon wiggled the bar back and forth, loosening the dirt and prying the boulder free from its resting place, he looked critically at the rock. At least on this side, the stone wasn't cozied up against a second one. Which most of the bigger rocks so far had been.

Brendon probed for another edge, then brought the digging bar down again.

*Ting.* The tip of the digging bar sent off a puff of smoke as it hit a hidden edge of the rock.

"Dang it," Brendon cursed under his breath, his arms still jittery with the force of the blowback.

Again, what a difference a few weeks had made. Before, Brendon couldn't hit the rocks hard enough to make the digging bar smoke. Dad had told him that sooner or later, they'd spalled off enough inches from the digging bar that they'd have to replace it. Somehow.

Brendon put down the digging bar and picked up his shovel, scraping around the dirt to find the other edges of the stone.

"Dad?" Brendon called after he got a better look at the rock. He waved his father closer.

Dad walked from his end of the old soccer field they were removing the rocks from. They were each clearing a three-foot swath of land, supposed to meet in the middle. Dad was much farther along his patch than Brendon. But he was a lot older than Brendon's fourteen years. Plus, he had more experience clearing this land, as he'd already spent all spring in a different corner of the former field, getting rid of the rocks there so they could plant a larger crop.

They'd quickly learned that fields that used to be farmed, once upon a time, were too open. *Myst* could swirl up there without warning, spoiling a season's crop in less than an hour, as well as making the land infertile. So they had to clear new land and farm in strips with walls and hedges in between, strips that curved and stopped the *myst*.

The boulder Brendon had been trying to remove was oval shaped, about two feet long and a foot across. Most of it was gray-brown and mottled, perfectly camouflaged by the surrounding dirt.

However, Brendon had struck one edge of the stone with enough force to chip off the outer layer of rock.

The gash wasn't white or gray, or even the orangeish red of the iron-ore rocks he sometimes found.

No, under the dirt and the first layer of stone was a pretty, pale blue layer.

Did it go all the way through the rock?

Dad merely grunted when Brendon showed him the stone. "Saw a few of these in the far field," he said, obviously unimpressed.

"What kind of rock are they?" Brendon asked, smoothing his fingers along the crack.

"Some type of geode," Dad said. "I split a smaller one apart by accident. Different colors of blue running all the way through."

"Do you think they're worth something?" Brendon asked, eagerly standing up. Maybe they could make enough to hire workers so he could go back to school this fall, wouldn't have to spend all his time in the fields....

"They're not worth a thing," Dad said. He spat in disgust.

Had he tried already? Carted one of these heavy boulders into the closest town, maybe even all the way to Tukwilla, only to be laughed at?

At Brendon's crestfallen look, Dad added, "One of the old men at the tavern called them dragon eggs. Said if the winter witch blessed them, they'd hatch into dragons."

Brendon sighed. "Dad. I'm not ten, you know." Dragons didn't really exist. Any more than fairies. Or witches. Or Santa Claus. And dinosaurs hadn't really lived with people, either.

Dad still smiled at Brendon. "Just telling you what was told to me," he said. He put his arm over Brendon's shoulder and looked out at the empty hulks of houses that surrounded what used to be a park—mostly looted, some burned out, two mysteriously just gone, as if a very precise tornado had stolen them away. Only Brendon's family house had been maintained, at the corner of the field.

"I know you'd rather be with your books, son," he said softly. "Hell, I'd rather be working in some kind of office. But since the bombs—"

"I know, Dad," Brendon said. And he *did* understand. All the kids did. Even when the adults tried to hide the truth.

That since the bombs two years before, nothing worked like it should. Not the electricity, not the chemistry, not the physics, nothing. The world had shifted in ways that people said were impossible. Rifts developed in odd places, where things best not spoken of thrived in the darkness.

Complaining about it didn't help.

They would just have to discover the new laws about the world. Create new order. New ways to do things. Find new laws and math and physics that allowed for the impossible.

No one had lives like they'd once had. A lot of places where people had lived weren't inhabitable anymore, particularly the cities. Sickly fog filled them—*myst*—poisonous and deadly. Rumors claimed the *myst* hid creatures from nightmares.

At least they stayed there. Brendon knew that the adults were worried about what happened *when*, not *if*, the creatures started spilling out.

So everyone made do and cleared areas that had never supported farms before like the huge soccer field that Brendon and his dad now cleared. The edges were lined with lines of salt—something that the *myst* avoided. They would patrol this field more vigilantly, make sure the lines stayed unbroken so the *myst* couldn't sneak through.

The newly formed enclaves had to rely on people like his dad who had a degree in agriculture but who'd moved to the city after he'd graduated and had spent most of his adult life away from the land. Who'd escaped the devastation just by chance, their family visiting cousins out in what Brendon had always called the sticks, though it really was just a suburb of Seattle.

"Let's get this rock out, then," Dad said. He squeezed Brendon's shoulders, then picked up the digging bar.

"All right," Brendon said. He held back his sigh. He still wasn't used to such work. But at least he didn't have the blisters he used to. His hands had healed and his muscles had built.

Not like there were any girls nearby for him to show them to. Not like he had any free time, either.

There did turn out to be another rock snuggled up against the blue boulder. Both Brendon and his dad dinged their shovels on it. But finally they were able to remove the boulder.

Brendon's muscles strained as he picked up the huge rock. Normally, he would just toss these boulders to the side, or build the hedge between this strip of land and the next. The edges of the new field were littered with them, as if they'd had a great battle with the stone.

This particular boulder, though, Brendon carried all the way across the rich earth and set on the side, closest to their home at the corner of the park.

He didn't believe in blue dragons or some type of winter witch. No matter how cool the idea of dragons sounded.

But there wouldn't be any harm keeping an eye out for them, either. Not since the world had changed.

# II

Haara danced with the golden motes spiraling down the sunbeam, circling, swirling, twirling her many skirts woven from cool shadow and moonlight. Not many sunbeams made it through the *myst*, as the humans called it. Haara drew what light she could to herself, sucking it like an old-fashioned hummingbird sipping at nectar, her head back, her long tongue licking the goodness out of the air.

Humans didn't know that hummingbirds were old-fashioned, of course. They hadn't realized yet that hummingbirds—like many of the other birds—now lived off the *myst*. They didn't understand how the birds had changed, becoming messengers and spies, and how they were no longer a friend of man.

Haara sighed as the *myst* shifted, cutting off her beam. She floated like a dandelion seed, her skirts spread wide, across the empty floor and to the edge of the broken window. Looked down the canyon formed by the other buildings. Somewhere beyond the blocks of buildings at the far end of the street lay the water, still. She could taste it in the air, though she had never seen the Sound, or been introduced to it. Her sisters had told her about it, however. How it would rise, soon. Take Seattle into itself.

The other buildings weren't all empty. No others held witches, though, not like her. No one else that looked so human—human-sized and human-shaped—with an overgrown skirt and useless legs dangling beneath.

Other creatures lived in those buildings, like the long-eared beagle that had eight legs and built extraordinary, beautiful webs out of lines of poetry, shimmering in the dark lights. Or the feline who blew smoke out from her tattooed fangs, long stories told with dancing shadows, fates that might have been, fates to come.

None of them were in the street. The sunbeams made them shy. They were of the night, and took substance from the shadows. Not like her. Not a summer witch, longing for stray sunbeams.

Haara turned back from the concrete-and-vine-filled canyon, back toward her room.

There had been furniture there, in her building, once. Ugly boxes made from scratchy, generic cloth and cold metal. Rolling chairs that belonged in torture chambers, not offices.

One of Haara's first sisters had broken the windows. Others had started pushing everything out, clearing out the building floor by floor. Haara had finished the job, delighting in the tinkling of the broken glass, the way the desks had tumbled gracefully through the air, splintering into ten thousand pieces when they hit the concrete below.

Like her sisters before her, Haara had explored the entire office building. Up to the very top, which was too exposed to the *myst* and the air and the non-birds. Down, down, through floor after floor of empty offices. The lobby that once held mere plants but now grew a jungle. To the basement where the hulking beasts human once drove rusted and dissolved, like sugar cubes melting in the rain.

Haara knew there were things she was supposed to do. Patterns she needed to find. Webs she should weave to hold back the *myst* so more sunbeams might poke through. She should grow her building stronger, poofing out the lower levels so it more resembled her dandelion skirt. Give it a chance against the coming Sound.

But there was another sunbeam, dancing in the far corner. Haara floated over to it, her legs dangling, as useless as the teats that still took up much of her chest. She'd never suckle a babe.

Haara gave a trilling call as she danced in the new beam, circling and licking, gathering more power to herself. There would be time enough, later, to do all the things that needed doing.

She was the summer witch. She had all season. Fall was a long ways away.

# III

Sizoon sighed as her office building shuddered again. It was autumn, now, and the tide had come in. The Sound had been threatening for some time now to come ashore and drown the concrete canyons of the structures that once made up downtown Seattle.

And come it had. Not creeping subtly, no. But surging, wave upon wave, each stacking up, one upon the other, as if the waves were made of concrete, not water.

If only her sister Haara had built up the building more! Fortified the lobby to withstand the onslaught. Billowed out the concrete and metal beams, so the water could only go so high and not higher.

But Haara had wasted her time chasing sunbeams, licking away at the golden nectar flowing down them.

Sizoon did have to admit that she felt strong. Stronger than her previous sisters, or the other autumn witches. Haara had supped well, then not done anything with all the energy she'd acquired. Just danced her time away.

So now Sizoon, the autumn witch, was left holding the bag, having to do all the things her predecessor hadn't done.

Except that Sizoon had been born far too late in the siege against the Sound. Her building wouldn't survive. Oh, Sizoon could fight for a while. Fortify the I-beams. The plants in the lobby were all underwater, but she could still turn them, make them grow *for* her, not against her.

But this wasn't the place that Sizoon should be. It had been good enough for her sisters. To nurture them. Help the transformation. Give them a safe place from which to find their way, their new lives, changing dramatically with every season.

Her skirts were bigger, now. No longer like a single dandelion seed, but soft and wide, like an entire flower gone to seed. Her useless legs still dangled, even skinnier now, more like flower stamens. Her breasts had (finally!) gone away, with nipples more like pebbles.

Her teeth were still as sharp, her tongue just as long. And she was still the size of a small human woman. She just appeared taller because she floated.

However, Sizoon didn't get as much nectar out of the sunbeam as her sister had. She was sure of it.

She needed something else. She was the autumn witch. Not the summer witch.

But what?

Sizoon floated closer to one of the broken-out windows. She'd tried creating a web, like what the dog-man spun with his eight legs. Something to keep the whispering water out.

However, while the web she managed was pretty, it was far from waterproof. It did hold the *myst* at bay. And it gave her something to lean against, rubbery and sticky, as she pushed out over the concrete canyon below her and examined the progress of the Sound.

Looking uphill, yes, the water had crept higher. It had made it to the library and was now absorbing all the knowledge kept there, swimming in ink and words.

The Sound might turn into a philosopher, answering the deep questions, given time enough. If it could be bothered to talk to someone other than itself. Water was selfish. Even more so than witches.

Downhill was the same. More water piling into concrete canyons, creeping up the buildings, battling to dissolve everything in its wake, taking into itself all the secrets that had been there, the memories of life and commerce.

Debris floated in the water below Sizoon. Splinters of the desks her sisters had smashed. Foam from office chairs bobbed as if trying to swim to a non-existent shore and save itself. Plants and trees struggled to survive as themselves, individuals, and not as part of the great Inner Sea.

Dying plants.

Sizoon lifted her head. Race memory supplied the smell of an autumn forest—rich mulch and dried leaves, the sweet scent of pines and their soft blanket of needles.

Sizoon was the autumn witch. The Sound was colorless, flat, gray and black, empty.

Where could Sizoon find the colors of autumn?

Quickly, Sizoon raced to the top of her office building, looking beyond the wreck of the city and out to where the humans still toiled.

There. To the south. Though the woods had changed. They wouldn't be friendly. The trees were more alive now. They'd grown tired of man and industry and *progress*. They'd protect themselves better now.

But they weren't full of the *myst* yet, weren't birthing too many strange creatures.

Sizoon didn't want to leave the city. Her sisters had been born in this building. Every one of them had died there, too.

But the Sound was relentless. Her building would be taken. Soon.

After one last long flight, a goodbye to the shattered glass that still haunted the insides of the windows, the great empty spaces that once held men and his things, the plants struggling to breathe water, the *myst* holding back the sky, Sizoon did what none of her sisters had ever even imagined.

She started in one corner on the roof of her building, then flew, as fast as she could, to the other.

And beyond, off the edge of the building.

Winds caught at her billowing skirt. They pushed her along, and Sizoon clapped her hands in excitement. She was finally going! Doing something none of her sisters had even dreamed of.

Then a second wind pushed her and she found herself drifting back toward her building, as if she floated on a great tide.

With a heavy sigh, Sizoon dropped and tried to find another favorable wind. She didn't want to use up all her energy flying.

Another wind gushed at her, from the side, trying to knock her over.

Sizoon struggled to stay upright. She looked at her old building with fondness, then turned herself around, caught a better wind, and pushed forward again.

It was going to take longer than Sizoon had planned to reach the city's edge. It would also take all her strength and endurance to keep herself upright, to push against the winds, to find that one true course and stick to it. Make her way to the woods just beyond.

Maybe Haara hadn't been useless after all, gathering all that strength and supping up all those sunbeams. Sizoon might end up using all of the energy her sister had gathered, long before the autumn was over.

# IV

Brendon faithfully followed after his dad, double-checking the windows and doors, making sure the house was locked and secured against the night.

In exchange for an entire container of dill they'd grown and dried, the local artist/shaman had come and painted a complicated sigil just inside the door. She'd done it in black, with swooping lines that feathered out on one side, and closed eyes in the center.

Every night, Dad traced over the design using bright pink chalk. Brendon checked it carefully after Dad finished, making sure that none of the lines were broken.

One set of eyes, or looking just once, was never enough against the *myst*. All of them had learned that they needed to check everything twice. Make sure the fine lines of salt ran unbroken along each window sill. That the rowan branches tacked above the doors were still fresh, the hawthorn berries unspoiled.

People had fallen back on the old ways, the old myths, for protecting hearth and home. Some worked, like salt and rowan wood. Some didn't, like daisies and belladonna.

Dad had only been fooled once, thinking a line unbroken when it wasn't.

The *myst* hadn't crept far into the house. With candles, a mound of salt, and a twig broom, they'd kept it confined all night to a single corner where it gibbered madly to itself.

In the morning, the wooden floor where it had stood was badly stained, as if tar had been left to dry there. At odd times, that corner still whispered to itself, hissing words that Brendon could never quite catch. Strange winds blew from it sometimes too, carrying the smell of the ocean.

However, though it hadn't come farther in, that had been enough. Mom had never been the same. She took to her bed after that, too afraid to leave, always complaining that the shadows pinched her if Brendon or Dad ever let the candles go out in her room.

Brendon barely remembered a time without the *myst*, now, though it hadn't been much more than four years before. When he could flip on a switch and light would flood a room. When hot and cold water came out of the taps, instead of the smell of rust and spiders. That seemed more like magic than what was creeping out of old Seattle, out of the *myst* and into their homes and fields.

Adults still sometimes denied what was before their very eyes. Brendon didn't understand it. Couldn't they *see?* Dad talked about them sometimes, how they couldn't adjust. Like Old Thomas. He'd said what was happening was impossible. The world didn't work that way.

Those adults sometimes didn't live for long.

Like Old Thomas. He'd been found dead on his living room floor, all stretched out as if ropes had bound his hands and feet, drawing him to the different corners.

Brendon wasn't sure if the smile Old Thomas had worn had made it better or worse, a maniacal grin which made it look as if he'd giggled himself to death.

Once the house was secure for the night, Brendon went up the stairs to his bedroom. Dad and Mom had converted the den downstairs for their own bedroom. They worried about him sleeping so far away. But Brendon insisted. He couldn't sleep down there.

He couldn't explain how he relished the emptiness of the upstairs. How the open space appealed to him.

Adults were much more afraid of the open, now, of wide clear spaces where *myst* might collect, pool and form another sinkhole, spoiling a field and making the area uninhabitable. Another portal for things that went bump in the night. Their own fields now curved around trees in the center, small piles of rocks, hedges of blackberries, anything to break up the straight lines that the *myst* liked to race along.

Of course, the woods weren't much better. The *myst* got hung up in the trees, like midnight spiderwebs, cold and slimy, smelling like moldy seaweed, as chilling as the bricks in the winter.

But upstairs was safe enough. Brendon had shut off the other rooms, blocked the door jambs with salt and rowan wood, willow switches tacked up over the doorways, chalk designs drawn on the floors. He checked them every night just to make sure, going in a great, clockwise circle, then checked them again, being his own second set of eyes.

On nights when the wind sang particularly loud and carried eerie sounds, he checked them a third time as well.

The big open room, where Brendon had vague memories of watching movies with his parents, was where he stayed at night. He'd pulled out the couch (strong enough from working the fields to do it himself) and dragged in his bed. He could see the rest of the farm from there; the well-protected fields, the dark edges of the woods, and the glittering of the first frost, though in previous years, it never got this cold this early.

But the weather had changed too, the winters growing deeper, more bitter, while the summers were hotter.

The weather was the least of their worries most of the time.

Brendon told his dad that the rocks he'd called dragon eggs worked as well as salt for protecting the land. He'd watched the *myst* come creeping out of the great corridor, only to be repelled by the rocks.

Dad hadn't seen it, though, and hadn't been willing to take a chance that Brandon was right. He still insisted on more salt and rowan saplings to line the edges of the fields they'd worked so hard at clearing. Which meant more money and goods going out of the farm, instead of coming in.

Tonight, with the full moon, the trees shook their heads, driven by winds that never touched the house. Lines of light flashed across the sky—like heat lightning, though there was no storm. Even through the closed window, Brendon smelled cinnamon and sage, salt and dried leaves, the cold coming winter and imminent changes.

Brendon didn't tell his parents about the creatures who came out of the trees, or were blown on the winds. Or any of the adults, really. They were convinced that everything that came out of the *myst* was evil.

The other kids his age, they knew about the other beings, the ones who weren't evil, but who helped. They'd seen. But they kept them secret among themselves. Not that he spent a lot of time with other kids—there was always too much work to be done.

Like the cat woman with great fangs that glowed with brilliant violet designs, as if they'd been tattooed. She blew smoke that pushed back against the *myst*, stopped cold any creatures creeping out of it.

Or the dog man with long ears and eight legs who spun webs that melted in the morning light, leaving behind patches of land that were noticeably more fertile.

Or now—the dandelion woman—who danced with the blowing leaves. They whirled under her skirt, puffing her up as she swayed on the wind, circling and dipping. The orange, yellow, and red of the leaves glowed more brightly in the moonlight as she danced with them. However, by the end of her dance, they'd all be brown, crumbled and faded. Sometimes all that remained were the spiderweb vein structures.

Brendon thought she was beautiful, though he didn't understand why. Her teeth were merely sharp points. She had no legs, just strings that dangled under her skirt.

However, her face shone with a fierce joy that set Brendon's heart pounding.

There were fewer leaves for her to dance with tonight. The trees had lost most of their fall colors, and now stood as mere bare branches against the late fall sky. *Myst* dripped from the bare branches, like pieces of night made solid and real.

Soon, it would be winter. Brendon didn't know what would happen to the dandelion woman. She always grew bigger, stronger, during her dance with the leaves.

When all the leaves had fallen, and all the colors drained away, what would she do?

# V

Kireen rested (*merely rested, not collapsed, no*) on the ground under the trees, her large dandelion skirt folding around her. She couldn't sleep there. Could. Not.

Sleeping on the ground was dangerous. The *myst* would come.

Or worse, things out of the *myst* would find her. The creatures would let her be. But vines would creep out. Tangle in her skirts. Violate her. As it had her sisters.

Kireen forced herself up, away from the ground, into the air. She swayed there, exhausted. Where were the soft fall breezes to pick her up? The winds were now too cold to support her multiple skirts.

And the leaves, oh her beautiful, colorful leaves, had all disappeared. She'd sucked every lick of color out of them. All the hot oranges that steamed her blood, the reds that warmed her nights, the yellows that cooled her days, even the browns that helped her clear the air. They were all drained. All gone.

Kireen dipped in the air, the minor strings of her former legs dragging on the ground. She couldn't stay here among the trees. She had to get out. Away.

But where?

The woods, the trees were her life. They provided her with life. They'd been her savior, her comfort, her home, for her entire life, since her foolish sister the summer witch had passed.

However, there wasn't anything here for her. Not anymore.

Kireen needed out. It was the same driving need, like right after she'd been born, when she'd had to leave the sky and the sunshine and descend into the woods. She must leave the trees. Get free of their cover. Out under the moonlit sky. Maybe find more leaves to dance with.

Kireen pushed herself again. Why did she always have to be the one who pushed? She bitterly resented the easier life her previous sisters had lived in Seattle, with the grand office building that had been once been theirs.

Now, Kireen fought to breathe under the trees. Vines stretched between the limbs, trying to catch her, alter her flight. Empty branches above her obscured the sky. She couldn't see the stars. The smell of rotting mulch, leaves already turning to dirt, floated up to her.

A vine reached up to snag Kireen's skirt. She tugged at it, trying to get away. The edge of the woods was just there. She couldn't lose all the energy she'd built up over the fall during a stupid fight. What would her sisters say? She pulled harder, trying to get away. But the vine held fast.

Finally, Kireen made herself look down, afraid of what she'd see.

The vine was ugly, spiked like a blackberry bush but without any sweetness, no berries or flowers. Instead, it had a claw-like hand, with nails long and black, dripping with sticky sap. Slowly, the hand tangled more and more of her skirt, the fingers picking at the dandelion-like seeds, pulling them together.

She had to get away. She couldn't lose her skirt. She wouldn't be able to fly. And what the vine would do to her, when it touched her skin....

Then the vine grabbed one of her legs.

Kireen screamed, but it wasn't enough to deflect the pain. It was worse than broken glass being scraped across her skin, an image from one of her sisters who'd lived in Seattle.

God, was she going to have to tear her own leg off? She would. She gulped, finding it hard to breathe through the pain.

Kireen shuddered and struggled wildly to get away. She thrashed, flew up, down, from side to side.

But the vine held on. Tightened its grip. Climbed higher.

Kireen noticed a single patch of leaves below her. A few spare, errant, yellow elm leaves tucked in among the brown.

She ducked down suddenly, surprising the vine. Before it could get a tighter grip on her, Kireen picked up the leaves. Using the edges like razors, she cut at the vine, hacking it apart. Her arms ached with the effort. She was using too much energy. She'd never make it out of the forest.

Finally, though, the vine let go. With one last sudden push, sucking out the final color from the leaves she held, Kireen flew out from under the trees, into the open air, cursing herself.

She'd rested too long, been too enamored with her leaves. Like Haara and her other sisters before her, she hadn't done what she was supposed to do, despite having all season long.

Now, it was too late.

Kireen drifted to the field, carried by errant winds—really, she was barely flying, now.

Rocks rested on the side. The blue rocks that had always attracted her.

She knew now that she should have done something with them. Shared her power. Made them grow. Helped the poor humans in their battle with the *myst*.

Kireen floated down on the soft breeze that carried her, landing lightly on the blue rocks.

She couldn't bless them. She felt bad about that. She told herself that maybe it wasn't time for them to be blessed, but she suspected she was lying to herself.

She breathed her last on them, frosting the gray outward rock, heating up the blue core, but not enough. Not enough to make them grow as they should.

Kireen passed away then, losing herself in the welcoming darkness, fading with the last of the dancing leaves.

# VI

Brendon watched from his high window, fascinated by the dandelion woman. He'd seen her before, the previous fall, as well as the fall before that, spiraling up above soft whirlwind of leaves under a full moon. He could tell she was hurt. One of her legs trailed far beneath her, as if it had been stretched. She didn't drip blood from her skirt, but it was ragged, the dandelion bloom no longer even.

She'd fought something, probably a creature from the *myst*, and had barely gotten away.

Graceful as always, the dandelion woman floated down onto the blue rocks. Her skirts billowed out over them, covering them with down.

The woman part of her swayed back and forth, blown by winds that nothing else could feel. Then she collapsed to one side, her arms losing their shape as her head dropped down.

Brendon blinked, surprised.

Was she dying?

There was no way he could go out and help her. He wouldn't open the house to the *myst*. Who knew what would attack him if he left the safe confines of their blessed home?

But she was dying. She sighed once, twice, her body fluttering up, her arms hanging down, her eyes glassy white.

Then she died.

Brendon found tears pricking his eyes. He'd never met the dandelion woman. He still knew she was special. Not one of the dangerous creatures from the *myst*, but an ally of sorts.

Brendon put his head down on the sill (careful not to disturb the line of salt there) and breathed deeply.

He wouldn't cry, couldn't shed tears for her. There were too many things broken, the world around him dying, for him to cry anymore.

When Brendon looked up, the dandelion woman had changed. Her brown skin had grown white, as pale as new snow. Her skirt had fluffed out again, more full than it ever had been.

When she raised her head, Brendon couldn't help but notice the differences. Her teeth were still sharp points and her chest was more like a man's. Her face was harder now, the angles sharper. Her chin was more pointed and her nose stuck out farther. Her eyes were blue instead of brown, the same blue as the insides of the rocks she lay on.

Was this the winter witch? Her skin was so white, and her skirt glowed with light all on its own.

Was the winter witch born from the fall witch every year? Were there also spring and summer witches? He'd have to watch for them more carefully.

If this was the winter witch, had she come to bless the blue-dragon-egg rocks?

Or would dragons hatch from the rocks she'd been born on?

The winter witch floated up, light as a moonbeam. The winds around her sparkled. She reached down with one graceful arm and spread frost from her fingers across one of the gray mottled rocks.

Then she touched a second and a third, freezing them solid. Blessing them with her cold breath.

Was just her touch enough to hatch the blue dragons?

The winter witch drifted higher, floating up above the rocks, her head tipped back. Winds caught at her skirt and she danced, slowly revolving above the protected field, the heads of the last of the winter wheat bowing in obeisance.

Brendon held his breath when she appeared to notice the house. But she didn't come any closer.

Did she see him? Recognize him? Did she know that he was the one gathering the rocks? Her eyes bored into him, just for a moment, before she floated away, above the dark trees.

Brendon would go and check the blue-dragon-egg rocks in the morning. Would they be the same? Or would they be different, somehow? Warmer, stronger?

Brendon vowed to collect as many of the blue dragon eggs as he could. Every rock he could find. He'd build her an altar, a temple, a tower made out of the blue-dragon-egg rocks.

So she would come back. Bless them some more.

Maybe bless the rocks enough that they would hatch.

# VII

Leluree knew there was something she was supposed to do. Something about the rocks. Something that her sister Kireen had left undone, too busy dancing with the leaves.

At least she'd left Leluree with *some* energy, though it was just a tiny bit. And Leluree would need all the energy she could get to survive the coming cold.

The winter would be harsh this year. Snow and ice promised to coat the world for long months.

But the frost…ah, the frost. So beautiful to paint all over the ground. Graceful lines to mark her dance. Cold winds that tickled her feet, fed her.

Her skirt was full, and would be fuller still, to match the spreading whiteness of the season.

She glanced down at the rocks beneath her. The rocks the young man had gathered, the one watching from the house. She was supposed to do something with those. Maybe she would remember, later.

For now, she was going to dance. Let the winter winds fulfill her. Ice would come later, sink into her skin. And snowflakes as well.

But for now, there was just the dance.

# VIII

"Don't I tire you out enough working in the fields?" Dad commented to Brendon as he trundled by, carting another wheelbarrow full of the blue-dragon-egg rocks to the field closest to the house. The late summer sun hung low in the sky, still burning, though the evening air blowing out from the trees was cool. Green crops filled the fields, growing in curved lines between the barriers they'd set up to confuse the *myst,* prevent it from pooling and gathering, sucking the life out of their plants.

"Believe me, Dad, you work me hard enough," Brendon assured him. He was always exhausted. Always longing for a nap or sleep or even maybe a day off. Always hungry, too—he *was* still a teenager, though only for half a year more. There still never seemed to be enough food.

However, gathering the blue-dragon-egg rocks was important. The winter witch hadn't blessed them that past winter, nor the winter before. But she would, someday. Brendon *knew* it.

This last winter had been a bad one. The snow had been deeper and the cold more severe than any winter in recent memory.

The winter witch that year had struggled to fly through that bitter cold, as if the winds fought her instead of supported her. She obviously preferred the more temperate nights, when there was just frost and moonlight. Then she'd glowed brightly as she danced across the fields, spraying out her own special frost that Brendon knew would sink through the snow as it melted, make the fields more fertile come spring.

Brendon prayed that the winter witch would bless the rocks, fully charging them, hatching the dragons buried within. They'd help Brendon and all of Lakeland fight the *myst.*

He didn't know how he knew that, but he just did.

All of the witches seemed to like the tower that Brendon was building. They would all rest on it, sometimes for most of a night.

However, the winter witch would just stare at it and never rest there. During the past winter, she reached out and touched the rocks only twice, spreading her magic across them.

Brendon was determined to build the tower higher that summer. That way, when the winter witch came again, she wouldn't have to fly down very far in order to touch the rocks. To bless them.

To change them into something else.

Dad just shook his head as Brendon continued on his way, but he didn't say anything else. Didn't offer to help either, though.

It was now just the two of them. Mom hadn't survived the darkest nights that past winter.

The corner of the dining room, where Brendon and his dad had trapped the *myst* that one night, stayed very quiet for more than a week, no sighs or whispered words or strange smells coming from it.

Was it in mourning? Missing the human that it had tortured the most?

However, then it came back, louder than ever, hissing its disappointment frequently.

Dad had talked about moving, but to where? It wasn't as if they could afford to either build a new house, or fix up one of the existing hulks of the old houses. They had to be near the fields.

Brendon carefully put his rocks into a sling, then climbed the ladder he'd set up so he could pile them at the very top of the tower. Soon, he was going to have to either build a taller ladder, or make a platform and another ladder.

The rocks didn't look special, not on the outside. The tower looked gray and brown, and smelled like dirt.

However, Brendon no longer had to scrape a rock with his knife to know if blue existed on the inside. He had to only touch it to know. He hadn't trusted his ability at first, had always double-checked. When he discovered he was one hundred percent accurate, he'd quit checking, and just let his hands guide him.

This was something else he didn't share with anyone.

He also knew Dad thought he'd lost his mind. Some of the neighbors did as well. Had any of them seen the winter witch? It wasn't something people talked about. The adults were certain that everything that came out of the *myst* was evil. And while the witches had probably been born in the *myst*, they weren't evil. Brendon was sure of it.

Just as he was certain that some year, the winter witch would spend enough time with the blue-dragon-egg rocks that they would hatch.

# IX

Jayzene floated high above the earth, drunk on sunshine. Green fields spread out beneath her, broken apart with islands of trees and rocks, curving in ways that were natural, not looking man-made.

The humans were learning how to keep out the *myst*. But it wasn't enough. She and her sisters all held that knowledge. War was coming.

War the humans might lose, once the *myst* found its champion.

But Jayzene didn't want to think about that, the cold winds, the deadly creatures, the dark days and nights that lay ahead. Instead, she focused on the sunshine, and how much she could absorb out there, away from the city.

Yes, she missed their old building in Seattle, the one that her sisters had let slip into the Sound. It had been safer there. She could afford to rest, to *sleep*. Creatures weren't always waiting to pounce on her, pull her down, rip her skirts, steal away her energy for their own.

But the sun, oh, the glorious sunlight! It filled her with so much power. So much *potential*. It gave her the strength to keep moving through every night, to only sleep a tiny bit every day, a few winks here and there.

Jayzene hadn't wasted that energy, unlike her sisters. She *had* remembered what she was supposed to do. At least, sometimes.

She'd discovered that she could trap sunlight around the edges of the woods, wrap it soundly between the edges of the trees and keep the *myst* at bay. It made that section of the trees safe and helped the humans in their fight to survive.

Maybe Jayzene could do more. There were those rocks, piled up on the edge of that one farm, a tower growing tall. They called to her sometimes, a soft whistling sound, promising safety, a sweet respite from always having to fly and move so the *myst* couldn't catch her. The human there had built a high, steady wall that circled in on itself with the perfect perch for her and her sisters, a wide expanse for her skirt to billow out around her.

She *was* safe there. Safer than anywhere else she'd discovered, except this high in the air. The birds might spy on her here, but there wasn't anything they could do to her. Not even the hummingbirds.

However, there was a price to pay for such safety.

The rocks also wanted their toll, sipping off her energy, channeling it into themselves. Not a lot, but any seemed like too much sometimes. They were growing…growing what, she couldn't quite say. It wasn't for her to bless them, but her sisters.

So Jayzene resisted the siren's call of the rocks and floated far above the earth, making her sunlight traps when she remembered, dancing with sunbeams the rest of the time, gathering as much energy to herself as she could.

There wasn't really anything else for a summer witch to do, was there?

# X

"So whatcha building out in that field of yours?" Duncan asked as Brendon stared into his beer.

Brendon looked up. People had asked before. He'd always just told people it was a wall. To help keep the *myst* out. And each person had laughed at him, knowing it was impossible.

He'd told Duncan his story before. But the question seemed different this time. More pointed.

The tavern was full that afternoon, all the benches taken up with the remaining young men and women who'd worked all morning and had called off early that afternoon, looking for a little beer or mead, or even wine from past seasons before the winters had gotten too cold for the vines to survive. Sunlight still poured through the front windows, just beyond the wooden bar. No one would linger into the dusk of the afternoon— better to be safe at home, behind salt-laced doors and blessed windows.

Almost all of them had lost their parents in the last year. It seemed that no one past the age of forty survived for very long in the new world. No one knew why. They'd all just fallen, one by one, generally in their sleep.

Brendon and the others were now the adults, though Brendon had just turned twenty-one. Merely six years since the rifts and the *myst* had formed.

He barely remembered the old world anymore. Remembering or even reminiscing about the old ways wasn't useful to their survival.

"What do you mean?" Brendon asked carefully. It wouldn't do to appear to be too odd. Not these days. Men and women sometimes went *wyrd*, spouting gibberish then attacking other people before they took their own lives. Folks speculated that the *myst* had gotten to them somehow. Or that they'd listened too closely to the *myst*.

He'd seen the looks they gave Terri, the local shaman/artist. Knew that some folks wouldn't let her near their kids. Afraid her power would turn her *wyrd* as well.

"That tower. With the rocks," Carlson said, coming up behind Duncan.

"Eh. It's a wall. Keeps the *myst* out, you know?" Brendon said. "Been building it for a while." He tried to keep his tone casual, but he was well aware of how far he was sitting from the door. How intently everyone was watching him. How this all had the feeling of being planned.

They wouldn't suddenly declare him *wyrd*, would they?

"We seen that," Duncan said, nodding. "But it ain't like any wall we seen before. And you keep adding to it. Why?"

Brendon looked at Duncan, at Carlson behind him. The others, like Ed and Stephan and even Bridget, who was as tough as any of them. Good people, strong, solid. Willing to help pitch a roof when necessary, or clear a new field.

All of them old before their time, thrust into adulthood whether they were ready or not.

The *myst* had been gaining strength that fall, winds constantly howling and tearing at them. Sudden fear made Brendan stop sometimes, glance over his shoulder at the nearby trees and shudder, though he couldn't see anything there.

*Something* was growing in the woods, something that none of them dared face.

The previous year, they'd tried burning down the closest parts of the woods, but the fires just went out. They couldn't keep them lit.

Then that night, the fires reappeared in their own barns.

They weren't winning the battle against the *myst*. They were just barely holding on. None of them talked about going back and retaking the cities, unlike their parents.

However, the older generation were all gone. Maybe it was time to talk of the things that were rarely spoken of, because the generation before them had never really *believed*.

Brendon started carefully. "You've seen the dog boy, right?"

Despite the sideways glances that people gave each other to see if their neighbors would admit it as well, most everyone nodded *yes*.

"Come to patch up my fields last month, after the *myst* broke through," Kerby admitted.

"Held back the *myst* when I expanded my fields last summer," Carlson said.

"And the cat girl?" Brendon asked, barely containing his excitement. He knew he hadn't been the only one to see them. He was relieved that others knew them as good.

"The Fanged One," Elizabeth corrected. "Who blows smoke from her great tattooed fangs to push back the *myst*."

"Stalks around this very tavern once every new moon," Bobby said from where he was standing behind the bar. "Keeps it a safe place to gather."

Everyone nodded again. Brendon felt his shoulders sag with relief. It had only been their parents who hadn't believed the good these creatures did. They'd been the only ones who proclaimed that all creatures who came out of the *myst* were evil.

"Then there are the witches," Brendon said. Surely the others had seen them, too. "They die and are reborn every season. They're attracted to the blue-dragon-egg rocks. I've been building them a platform."

"Do they help against the *myst*?" Duncan asked eagerly.

"You've seen the lighted portals on the edges of the trees, right?" Brendon asked.

"Been able to go a bit further into the woods because of those," Terry, the local shaman/artist said. "Makes it easier to gather the mushrooms, herbs, and and other things I need."

"Those come from the summer witch," Brendon said eagerly.

"I've seen those, too," Carlson admitted. "But I've never seen the creature who built them."

"All the witches have the same basic form," Brendon said, eager to finally be able to share his knowledge. "A dandelion skirt, thin strings for legs, sharp teeth. But the season dictates how white or brown their skin is, the color of their eyes, whether it's sunlight or leaves, frost or flowers, that powers them."

"And they like these, what, blue-dragon-egg rocks you've been gathering?" Ed asked.

Brendon nodded. "Someday, the winter witch will bless them. And they'll hatch. Into dragons."

Silence filled the room.

Brendon suddenly realized that he'd said too much. He needed to be more careful. Even with his neighbors and friends, the people in the community that he counted on. They needed to be able to depend on him as well. He couldn't show signs of going *wyrd*.

And talk of dragons hatching sounded crazy to them. He couldn't explain his gut feeling that the dragons would help against the *myst* someday.

"Here's to hatching rocks!" Duncan finally said, breaking the silence and holding his mug up in a toast.

Brendon gladly raised his glass with his peers, then felt further relief as the conversation shifted to the coming winter, as it often did, wondering if they had enough supplies laid in if it turned out to be another bad one. Commenting on how furry the caterpillars had been. Wondering about the thick nests some of the birds had built.

Brendon didn't think anything more about it until two days later when a crudely painted sign appeared at the edge of the lane leading to his fields: *The Blue-Dragon-Egg Farm*

Brendon angrily tore it down. Didn't they understand? At some point in the future, those rocks would be important. More important than the coming winter or The Fanged One.

When the sign came back the third day in a row, Brendon finally admitted defeat and paid for a professionally painted sign to be carved and put in its place. He made sure that the edges poofed out on both the top and the bottom in a dandelion design.

The next week, Brendon went back to the tavern. Of course, no one admitted to putting up the sign, though more than one of his neighbors specifically asked how the Blue-Dragon-Egg farm was doing.

Brendon was sure to laugh and to take the ribbing good-naturedly.

He also started checking with his neighbors, one by one, starting with Duncan.

None of them had ever heard of the legend of the winter witch. No one else had even seen the witches. They all had blue rocks, which they were happy to give them to Brendon. He started planning a rock-hauling service.

His dad, so many years ago, had said that an old man at the tavern had told him the legend. But who?

Had it been one of the witches in disguise? Someone else?

Some*thing* else?

# XI

Brendon married later that year, as much for necessity as anything else, especially after Jill had called a town meeting with chilling statistics, comparing Lakeland's birth and death rates.

At the change of every season, Brendon tried to watch the fields at night, to witness the death and birth of the new witches. He didn't always see the rebirth—either they transformed somewhere else, or it happened during a time when he was busy, like with the birth of his second son, Joshua.

But Brendon always saw the witches at some point during the season, dancing in the moonlight, blessing his fields and fighting the *myst*.

No one else in town ever admitted to seeing them. The witches appeared to primarily haunt Brendon and his burgeoning family.

When Brendon noticed his good neighbors who were merely a few years older than he was dying as they turned forty years old, he spent less time in the fields every day and more time talking with his children and anyone else who would listen, making sure they understood the importance of planting trees that had leaves that changed colors in the fall for the autumn witch, as well as flowers that would bloom for the spring witch.

It didn't matter if his heirs believed in the legend or not, if they called the blue-dragon-egg tower a folly, as his oldest son had mistakenly done once.

Though Brendon didn't remember believing in Santa Claus, or even the great Jesus, he knew the witches were real.

And someday, those eggs and the dragons contained within were going to save them all.

# Of Myst And Folly

## One

Joey waited and waited and *waited* for Grandpa Schuller to finish reminiscing about the good old days and place his rock with the others in the basket. The days when mythical cars ruled the trails, rolling along without horses or oxen. When planes—birds big enough to carry people—crisscrossed the waters, unafraid of what lurked below. When everyone had a kind of magic, and lights and water and heat would appear in someone's house with just a wave of their hand.

Da, Uncle Irving, and Aunt May had already finished with their speeches (thank The Fanged One, they'd been short) and had reverently placed their rocks in the basket already. They stood in their best clothes—black pants and vests, with white shirts—to one side, listening intently. The rest of the family circled the group, Ma and Joey's older brothers and his one sister and his cousins, spread out on the house-side of the first field, at the foot of the tower.

Once Grandpa Schuller finished, Joey, Mark, and Heidi would get to finish the ceremony: climb the tower, pull up the bucket, then place the rocks up top. It was the first year Joey was old enough to join the others, having just turned ten that spring. He looked up toward the top of the tower, soaring higher than their house, maybe as much as four stories tall.

Great-great-great (was it three greats? Or four?) Grandpa Brendon Schuller had put it in his will that stones must be added to the tower every year.

Not just any stones. Blue-dragon-egg rocks. The kind that looked normal on the outside—gray and brown—but had layers of bright blue on the inside.

The family legend held that the winter witch would bless them some winter, hatching the stones into blue dragons that would fight the *myst.*

The stones were getting more difficult to find. All the ones from the Schuller fields had been used already. The fields closest to theirs—the Hyus' and the Browns'—had all been cleared as well. For a while, the family had even had a rock hauling business, helping farmers clear their fields for less money as long as the Schullers got to cart away all the blue-dragon-egg rocks.

Not everyone in the town of Lakeland believed that the stones would hatch into something. Max, Joey's best friend, during their worst ever fight, had told Joey that the rest of the town called the tower a folly.

Joey knew Max was wrong. There was something to the stones. Something haunting about the tower. He could *feel* it.

Not that he'd ever told Max, though. It was dangerous to be different, for people to declare you *wyrd* and drive you out, into the woods. Where the magicians lived. Or they even might kill you!

Just beyond the tower, past the first curved row of wheat, stood a dark hedge of trees. Even in the bright fall sunlight it looked cast in shadows.

*Myst* dripped from the trees, like sickly white spider-webs. Dark things lived there, that gibbered and howled at night. Made sleeping impossible sometimes, making all the family mad. Creatures hid there, some that would just kill a body if they were lucky.

Even Joey could remember when the trees in the field closest to the house didn't hold *myst.* Which was what Grandpa Schuller was talking about still. How the world had changed. Before magic. Before *myst.* Before the small gods, like The Fanged One—with her cat ears and purple tattooed fangs—who blew smoke that dispelled the *myst* and protected the town and the surrounding farms. Before Beagle Boy—who spun webs with his eight legs that held back the *myst.*

Before the witches, who changed every season, each of them protecting the Schullers from the *myst* with her own special abilities.

Finally Grandpa Schuller drew to a close. He asked everyone to bow their heads in prayer.

"O white, winter witch. Hear our call. Come and bless these rocks this year when the snow flies. Hatch what is in them, to help us fight the *myst*. Scatter your frost on our fields so that they may be more fertile in the spring. Hear our pleas, and keep us safe. Amen."

"Amen," Joey automatically responded with everyone.

Then Grandpa Schuller pulled out his rock.

Joey gasped. It wasn't *right*. It wasn't a blue-dragon-egg rock. It was just a plain, ordinary rock.

Grandpa Schuller wasn't really going to put *that* in the basket, was he?

Joey looked around at the other adults, frantic. They had to stop him! He was going to pollute the tower! The winter witch would never bless it and the blue dragons would never hatch!

Before Grandpa Schuller could put the stone down, Joey surged forward. "Wait!"

Everyone froze, looking at Joey. He didn't care. He snatched the rock from Grandpa Schuller before he could place it among the others, sitting at the bottom of the basket.

Those rocks were all right.

This one wasn't.

"This isn't a blue-dragon-egg rock," Joey explained. He held the rock up with both hands for everyone to look at it.

Why couldn't they *see*?

Da came forward and took the rock from Joey. It was much bigger than his hand, but he still held it in one palm, bouncing it up and down first with one hand, then the other. He looked at Joey and nodded.

Did Da agree?

Then Da pulled a knife out of his jacket. With a quick cut, Da scraped through the outer layers of the rock.

It was merely gray underneath. Not blue.

Da held the rock up for everyone to see. "Joey's right. It isn't a blue-dragon-egg rock."

All eyes turned to Grandpa Schuller. "It felt right!" he said, feebly defending his selection.

Grandma Schuller came forward and took her husband's arm. "It's okay," she assured him, leading him away.

"But I can still work!" Grandpa Schuller protested as they walked.

"Yes, dear, but not in the fields anymore," Grandma Schuller said firmly.

Joey shivered. Men would be forced to stop working in the fields when they'd lost their sensitivity to magic and the *myst*. They wouldn't realize when a magical vine had snagged their pants and was eating its way through their skin, they wouldn't stop working when the spy birds came calling, scouting an area before the *myst* arrived.

Most men didn't live long after they left the fields, even with everyone looking after them. Would Grandpa Schuller be dying soon? Would the Forties take him, like they did most people?

Da looked at Joey. "You felt this," he said, holding out the stone to Joey, "from all the way over there," he continued, pointing to where the rest of the family was still standing, several feet away.

"Yes, sir," Joey said. It hadn't been a bad thing, had it? They weren't going to accuse him of being too different, were they?

"I'm glad you caught it," Da said firmly.

But Joey still felt as though Da's eyes watched him the rest of the day, and the other adults, too. He wanted to assure them that he wasn't growing *wyrd*, the *myst* hadn't started talking to him, had never spoken to him.

He was normal. Like them. Human. Just part of the family.

Joey checked his eyes, later that night in the old mirror in the downstairs changing room, spending time turning his face this way and that. His eye were still a pale gray-blue, set off by his tanned skin and freckles. His hair was blond from the summer sun and would grow darker that winter again. He was taller than he had been, but had yet to grow as tall as Da. Maybe in a couple summers.

Not a hint of gold lurked in his eyes.

However, the next day, Joey paid more attention while he helped bundle hay. He automatically stepped over the rabbit hole in the furrow, while his older brother Steve blundered right into it, swearing as he tripped.

Joey also knew, without looking, when the birds had gathered in the trees, long before the spotter came to warn them.

He was determined to hide his differences, though. No one had to know. He didn't have to become a magician and leave the farm, go and live somewhere outside of Lakeland because no one wanted him nearby.

And later that night, when the spring witch came again, and called to him from outside his window, he didn't go.

# Two

Mitch kept himself wrapped firmly around Hana. They sat in the middle of their tiny shack while the winds and the rain and the *myst* pounded at it, shaking the thin wooden walls.

They'd thought it would be safe. They'd lived in their shack most of the summer. Their tribe had finally figured out how to appease Ocean and pull the bounty from her without being casually killed. It took prayers, and time, and many sacrifices, but it was worth it.

When the traders came to their village next spring, the entire tribe would be *rich*.

But Mitch and Hana had wanted more. They didn't want to have to make the treacherous journey back inland when the fall rains came. They wanted to stay close to Ocean.

They'd both felt the water speaking to them, had been lulled by the sound of the waves, the soft feel of the air. They'd loved dancing on the sand as the sun rose over the water, casting long lines of fire from the horizon to the beach. As well as the cool nights with the moon shining down on them, blessing them from the sky.

The tribe had proved they could live there, live off the bounty provided by Ocean.

But not a single other member of their tribe had remained past their annual fishing and salt gathering season. They'd all gone inland, claiming it was safer there.

Safer under trees filled with *myst*, safer hiding in shadows than living free on the sand?

Mitch had sneered at them, Hana silently agreeing by his side.

Man used to live there on the east coast. There weren't any houses remaining, but a brick wall here or there showed where they'd once been.

Mitch and Hana walked freely beside Ocean, the *myst* trapped in the trees inland. Ocean didn't permit the *myst* to come closer. They were free to roam the sand. Free to live under a clear blue sky. Free to experience the night, see the stars free of fear. Free to laugh and dance with the gulls, Ocean's messengers.

After a delicious week of casually harvesting and drying fish and seaweed, filling shallow rocks with salt water to evaporate and leave behind fresh, rich salt, dancing in the waves to ease Ocean's anger while making prayers and sacrifices every morning, storm clouds had gathered on the horizon and refused to leave the sky. The air smelled acrid and *furious*. Rains lashed Mitch and Hana every morning, and the sun never showed her face above the water.

Should they leave? Try to make the overland journey on their own? But neither of them had touched enough magic to keep them safe, particularly overnight when the *myst* and its creatures roamed. They also trusted Ocean. Despite the unnatural state of the constant storms, they trusted Ocean to keep them safe, to keep the *myst* at bay.

For one glorious day, the clouds had disappeared, leaving behind the bluest sky either Mitch or Hana had ever seen. The sun had set the waves to sparkling. Even the sand was clear of debris, looking soft and smooth.

Mitch and Hana had danced late into the afternoon, almost to sunset, around the bonfire they started on the beach, thanking the Walking Vine Men who had helped their people by tying back the *myst*, and the Parrot Boy who dispersed the *myst* with his mighty wings, as well as Ocean, who had consented for them to stay.

With night came the storm.

Hana felt its power first. "Check the windows. And the door," she said as the wind started howling.

Mitch had already checked, following along after Hana after she'd drawn the sigil just in front of the door, stopping any from evil coming across the threshold. He'd also checked the two window sills, where an unbroken line of salt lay, mixed with rowan leaves and slivers of oak bark.

One set of eyes was never enough. The *myst* was tricky, and could fool a single person.

But Mitch went and checked again, Hana watching him carefully. Her dark eyes were huge in her face, showing the terror she felt.

"Hey, hey, it's okay," Mitch assured Hana, going and draping an arm across her shoulders after he'd verified that the obvious openings into their hut were defended. "It's just a storm."

Hana's head, buried against his chest, shook hard back and forth. "No. It isn't just a storm," she warned.

"What is it?" Mitch asked, wrapping his other arm around her and drawing her in closer.

"There's something out there," came the muffled words.

"Ocean will keep us safe," Mitch assured Hana.

"I don't think She can," Hana said, still shaking her head. "Not this time."

Howling winds started next, constant, never relenting. Hana went to sit in the very center of their hut, on the woven mat, folded up over her knees, rocking and mumbling prayers.

Mitch joined her, wrapping himself around her back, trying to give her as much comfort as he could.

Then the *myst* had started screaming. Mitch had never heard it so angry. It carried foul smells that drifted through the hut, of rotten eggs and deep buried places, repulsive odors from the long abandoned cities.

Rain pounded the roof and sides of their hut. Mitch and Hana had woven the walls of their hut from vines and broad leaves. It had mostly protected them from the rain during the previous storms.

But the rain wasn't coming straight down this time. Instead, the wind drove the rain before it and it seeped in through the cracks in the walls, cracks Mitch hadn't known were there, but that the rain was doing an excellent job of finding.

"At least in the morning, I'll know where to patch," Mitch said, weakly trying to joke with Hana.

She didn't appear to hear him, but kept rocking and praying.

Words now followed along with the wind. Words that neither Hana or Mitch had spoken.

Mitch wanted to stick his fingers in his ears so he wouldn't hear the words, but that would have meant letting go of Hana. He tried to say prayers instead, praying to Ocean, to the Walking Vine Men, to Parrot Boy, even to the ancient Jesus. He recited old myths about the ancient times with its cars and planes and cinema, snatches of conversations he remembered with Hana.

Trying so hard not to listen.

Everyone knew that if the *myst* started speaking to you, you were doomed.

Mitch found himself repeating, over and over again, "Go away. Go away. Go away."

But he felt as effective as a three year old telling his parents that he didn't want to go to bed yet.

Mitch sighed and held Hana tighter when the first floating thread of *myst* pushed its way through the walls. It didn't matter how sealed or protected their hut was. The storm had loosened the very walls, providing cracks for the *myst* to creep through.

"We don't want you," Mitch said as clearly as he could. He could barely hear himself over the howling wind.

The *myst* replied, but not with words, not even with what Mitch would have labeled a language. It was more of an impression, a feeling of curiosity wafting toward him.

*Why?*

"We're happy here, on our own. Go Away! Leave us alone!" Mitch shouted, louder this time.

The winds whipped his words away.

Loneliness came over Mitch this time. He'd never felt it so sharply before. It was as if he stood by himself on a tower of rock, surrounded by water, with no way to get down. No one could climb up to join him, either. He'd never see another human being, never talk to a person again. He was by himself, just him and the rock and the wind and the waves.

Was that how the *myst* felt? That alone? Was that why it kept trying to talk to people?

No. It had to be a trick.

Suddenly, Mitch felt trapped, confined on all sides, caged in. He had the image of being surrounded by trees that were growing, pressing in on him. He wouldn't be able to move, soon. The trees would trap him forever.

The *myst* didn't feel this way. either. It was just trying to find a way to get through to Mitch, to make him agreeable to the *myst*, to stop guarding against it. To let the *myst* in.

It was evil, and all the things that came from it were evil.

"No!" Mitch said, trying to keep his voice as firm as it had been, though terror now wrapped around his soul as more of the *myst* gathered, looking like a tattered white cloth hanging in the air.

"Yes," came the hissed reply.

But not from the *myst*. From Hana.

She turned in his arms and looked up at him. Her once beautiful black eyes had turned golden and the pupils had formed into slits.

Mitch realized that Hana had been sitting on a crack in the woven mat. It spread out, going across the dirt floor on either side. The *myst* had already gotten in, slipping through the earth.

It had taken her soul.

"Come with me," she sighed. A hand that had once held his was now a claw, tipped with thorn-sharp talons, black as night. The other hand rose up, the claws gently scratching his cheek. Her long black hair flared out, medusa-like, around her head.

"I can't," Mitch said sorrowfully. And he couldn't. It meant letting go of his humanity, letting go of his soul, and Mitch couldn't do that. Even if the *myst* promised him a long life, living forever with Hana by his side.

The *myst* lied. Hana was already gone. And he would not become a tool of the *myst*.

"Then we will just take you with," she said, her golden eyes blinking, a forked tongue now licking her lips in anticipation.

Mitch struggled to get away, then. Tried to escape the claws and fangs and *pain* that the *myst* visited on him.

But he was doomed, they both had been, leaving the tribe and living on their own. It wasn't safe for man alone.

In the morning, Ocean took the hut, washed the sands clean again, and rumbled to herself until the *myst* pulled back farther into the woods, the pact between them firm once more.

Until the next time, when Ocean let man near her again.

# Three

Abraham sat outside his trailer, sketch book in hand, as the afternoon waned. His cooking fire burned brightly before him, confined to its circle of stones. It flared once, but Abraham had forgotten about it. Again.

Instead, Abraham drew furiously fast in the oversized sketch book that took up all of his lap. He made his own charcoal that smudged *just right* as he drew, the images pouring out of him as his hand raced across the page: tall men wearing clothes that were once easy and cheap to make; a huge round wheel with seats that swung as it went around, that people used to ride in; horses pulling small metal chariots, each with a single driver, dressed in what looked like a sheet.

When Abraham looked at his drawings with a clear head, he'd realize he'd drawn the past. Even today, in his half-aware state, he suspected it was the past that had overwhelmed him.

Abraham hadn't met anyone who could foretell the future. Not even the most powerful of magicians could do that. He still examined all his drawings carefully, searching for clues in the past, what had caused the rifts and the *myst*, if there was some hint there that could return the bright future that had once been promised man.

Slowly, Abraham's sight returned to him, and instead of images, he saw his front yard again.

Someone stood there. A girl, not more than sixteen, waiting on the other side of Abraham's cooking fire. She was skinny—hadn't eaten enough recently. Her skin was as pale as if she'd spent most of her life indoors, instead of in the fields helping her parents, which was what most kids did these days. She wore a plain brown dress, obviously made from a single piece of material, with a rope knotted around her waist. Her brown hair was straight and long on one side, almost down to her neck, but hacked short on the other, up over her ear. It looked as if she'd started to cut her own hair with a knife, then grown bored before she'd finished the job.

She wasn't paying any attention to Abraham. Instead, she was looking out into the gathering night, darkness and *myst* growing beyond the cooking fire. So he drew a quick sketch of her, a lone figure in the corner of a busy page, looking out over the page for…something. Waiting. Anticipation drawn along every line.

Abraham couldn't recall ever wanting something as much as this girl *wanted.* Then again, he hadn't felt anything intensely for ages. Not since he'd started calling the magic regularly.

When Abraham put the sketch pad to one side, she turned and looked directly at him. Her eyes were brown, normal, human. Unlike his, which were now fully gold with oblong slots for pupils. Some had likened them to goat's eyes.

Unlike most, Abraham had been willing to pay the price of magic, willing to exchange who he'd been for what he would become. He'd called on magic often enough that he'd been changed by it, permanently.

"Hello," Abraham said. He stayed sitting. He didn't want to chase off the girl, whose eyes had grown bigger now that she saw his full face.

He recognized that she felt fear. Once, long ago, he might have known what she felt. Might even have been able to sympathize. But the magic had eaten away at his empathy, his ability to care.

Abraham wanted her to stay because he was curious, nothing more.

The girl stared hard at him, cataloguing his differences.

He didn't have horns. Not yet. Just white bony protrusions above his temples, stark against his dark skin. His face had grown longer over the years. He'd had to pull out a few teeth as his mouth had grown smaller. He still had a great sense of smell, despite how his nose had shrunk and his nostrils were now mere slits.

While Abraham could use magic to hide that he was no longer human, he didn't care enough to try.

Not a single person in any of the three towns nearby trusted Abraham. It was why he lived out here, on the edge of the woods. He'd carved a space out for himself, well warded against the *myst*.

However, the townsfolk still sought out Abraham regularly, though normally they traveled in the morning or the full light of the afternoon, when it was safer. They needed Abraham and his magic, the sigils he drew to guard their houses from the *myst*, the charms he made for new mothers to protect their babies, the blessings he gave the fields every spring, the protections he wove for the cattle.

The price Abraham asked for such services varied, but mainly, he wanted paper. Something fresh and clean to sketch on. He'd made his own, but it wasn't as good as the leftovers from the abandoned places.

When the townsfolk brought him that paper, it was generally browned with age, yellow and flaking. Abraham could easily cure that. Just like he could repair the tattered cloth from that time, if it was mostly pure and not mixed with *polyester*, a term Abraham learned from one of his sketching sessions.

Abraham wasn't afraid of the girl standing across from him. She appeared to be merely human. His eyes hadn't just changed color—he could see magic and other things as well. Plus, his campfire burned between them. It was easy enough to fling the flames where he wanted.

Would her hair burn at different speeds? The short versus the long?

The girl tried to speak, cleared her throat, then managed to croak out, "Hello."

"What are you here for?" Abraham asked.

"Can you…can you teach me to do magic?" the girl asked, the words tumbling over each other.

Abraham sat up straighter in his chair. "I could say yes. And take your goods and time. But I would be lying. Anyone who says they can teach you magic is lying."

"Oh," the girl said. She looked down, biting her lip.

Who had lied to her about such things? Was this what parents told their children now, to get them to stay away from magic? No one wanted their children to become a magician.

Did she look sad? Abraham decided that must be what her expression now conveyed.

Abraham looked beyond the girl, out into the evening. "It's late," he warned. "If you want to stay and talk, we can, but then you'll have to spend the night."

It actually didn't matter to Abraham if the girl stayed or if she left and dared the *myst* and died. But he knew that the townsfolk would be upset if he just sent her on her way. And he did want to stay in their good graces. There were still sketchbooks tucked away, hidden in attics or abandoned houses, that they could gift him with.

The girl nodded. "I knew I was coming too late to go back home tonight. Thank you for offering your hospitality," she added, shyly.

"And what would you have done if I hadn't?" Abraham asked, curious.

The girl blinked her eyes, startled, as if she'd never considered that possibility. "I would have gone home alone," she said. "I've walked in the dark before," she added defiantly.

Abraham shook his head but didn't say anything. "Stay there," he said. "Close to the fire." He didn't want the *myst* coming closer, tempted by her idiocy.

He rose swiftly from his chair, the girl watching him curiously. His limbs were all normal—no cloven feet or oddly bent legs, no talons or claws, just hands.

In the tiny shack, Abraham fetched bread he'd baked on his fire that morning, unleavened but flavored with rosemary, lemon verbena, and thyme. He also pulled out two dried sausages he'd been saving, the meat cured with sea salt and garlic, as well as apples he'd picked earlier that week.

The girl still stood outside, but she'd edged around the fire now, closer to the shack. She looked fearfully out into the darkness.

"The *myst*, is it always so loud out here?" she asked.

Abraham shrugged. He'd gotten used to it so long ago he didn't notice anymore. He divided their food onto two plates, pulled out a jug of clear water for them to drink from, along with another chair.

"I'm Abraham," he finally said as the girl sat.

"Oh. Oh! I'm Erin," she said.

Abraham knew better than to try to shake hands with her. He'd heard too many stories—mostly untrue—about how magic could be spread by touch.

They ate without talking, the fire cackling before them. Wind blew the trees around them, and in the distance, the *myst* talked to itself, whispering and moaning.

Only when the girl had finished eating did Abraham try talking to her.

"Magic exists in every person," he started out with.

The girl nodded. Good. So she at least knew some of the basics.

"It isn't a question of how much magic exists. Every person has the potential to do great magics. The question is always the price."

"Price?" Erin asked.

"Do a little magic, and maybe your eyes turn gold for a day or so," Abraham explained. "You can still talk with people. Still look and think like people. Can still mate and have children."

"Like the magics my mother did, with her herbs and sachets," Erin said, nodding.

"Exactly," Abraham said. He knew that a few of the towns' women created minor protection charms. They tended to avoid him—either scared of what they could become, or afraid he might think they were competing with him. He hadn't realized any of them had children, though.

"If you keep doing magic, keep using it, keep pulling in the power and the *myst*, it starts to change you," Abraham warned.

"Power from the *myst*?" Erin asked. "Magic doesn't come from the *myst*," she added scornfully.

"Did you come here to learn, or to teach me?" Abraham shot back.

The girl's eyes grew wide again. "I'm sorry, sir," she said.

Even Abraham could tell she wasn't sorry at all. "*All* power, all magic, comes from the *myst*. It isn't of this world. It isn't *normal* or human. I've looked enough in the past," he said, gesturing at the sketchbook still resting against his chair, "to know that before the *myst*, there was no magic. Everything you've heard about, the lights and running water, the heat and music, all came from man. *Not* magic."

Erin pressed her lips together tightly, as if she'd like to argue but knew she needed to be polite.

Abraham sighed and shook his head. Oh, the arrogance of youth! He remembered, too well, how he'd refused to listen to his elders. How he'd challenged the *myst*, walking at night between houses in the town. How he'd wanted to crow about his victories in the morning, how he scoffed at the adults and their fears.

"I've touched the *myst*," Abraham told the girl. "If you start to do magic, any magic, great or small, you'll touch it too."

"But the *myst* is evil!" Erin said.

Abraham fixed as cold a stare as he could muster on the girl. "Yes. It is. But in order to survive, we must work with it. Take a little bit of that evil into ourselves. Change it for good."

Or at least that was what he told himself that he did. Really, he didn't know anymore. Did he pull the *myst* inside him? Or was it already there, just waiting to be worked? Waiting to slice off another sliver of his soul, to steal away a bit more of his humanity?

Someday, Abraham wouldn't turn away from the *myst* when he should. And it would take him wholly. Only his sketchbooks would remain.

"But how do you do that?" Erin finally asked.

"This is why I can't teach you magic. Why no one can," Abraham stated flatly. "Every person needs to find their own way through the darkness. To come back to themselves after facing the *myst*. The magic is there. The *myst* is there. How it talks to you will be different than how I talk with it."

Every magician Abraham had ever talked with approached the *myst* differently. One had likened it to dipping her toes in a cool stream. Another had mentioned sliding over the ice.

For Abraham, it had always been like going from merely walking to running at super speed, like how his hand moved when he drew.

Most people didn't try to access what was in them. Many who did try failed, and grew *wyrd*, the *myst* taking them over.

Erin didn't have any other questions and stayed blissfully silent while Abraham puttered around his fire. She slept on the floor of his shack, the blanket he'd given her wrapped fully around her, and was gone before he woke in the morning.

Would Erin be back? He doubted it. She would probably be one of the lost ones, who would dare the *myst* when she shouldn't, who would get lost and never go home.

It wasn't until two days later that Abraham discovered she'd taken his sketchbook with him. Why had she done that? He was more curious than angry.

And even more curious still when he couldn't find any trace of her, not in any of the nearby towns. No girl named Erin lived anywhere close.

## *Four*

Joey waited with the other teens on the far edge of town, watching for the first of the traders, where the rutted road curved, just before it disappeared into the *myst* and trees.

The early spring air blew playful winds along his neck, making him draw his wool coat up tighter. At least his patched leather boots were warm, if not waterproof, and his hand-me-down wool pants were thick enough to repel the wind. Despite the sunshine and clear blue skies, it was still cool. Mud filled the holes in the road, destined to become dry and cracked when summer started.

They sat together on an old wall, Joey and Max, along with the girls, Susan, Han Lee, and Bridgette. Fields spread out on either side, fallow this year. Hedges, walls, and clumps of well-trimmed trees broke up the space into curving lines that *myst* couldn't gather in. Joey cast a critical eye at the arrangement. The field looked well-tended, but he'd watch the second, no, third hedge from the road. Something else might be growing there that the *myst* could corrupt.

"What do you think the traders will bring?" Han Lee asked, braiding her long black hair back out of her face and binding it tightly so the wind couldn't mess with it.

Joey had always thought she was the prettiest of all the girls, not that he'd say anything to her about it. And he'd *never* tell Max, who would tease him mercilessly.

"Salt," Bridgette proclaimed.

Of course. She was the most practical of all of them. Her dad had gone *wyrd* when she'd been very young, almost killing her and her mom. She never wanted anything to do with magic, and had very little imagination.

"Paper," Susan guessed.

The mill set next to the Wolf River could only grind grain. For a proper paper mill, they'd need to build a second mill, and there just weren't enough hands or time in the day to man it.

It wasn't that most people in the town used paper, anyway. No, Tess and the other magicians needed it for their charms and spells, the things that kept the town safe. Paper was always in high demand.

"Silver," Max said, not to be outdone. "And mercury."

Joey nodded. Both of those were needed, again, mostly by the magicians, though some of it would be used by their own blacksmith.

They turned to Joey, who tried desperately to think of something unusual, something unique, that the others hadn't thought of. Not exotic spices like nutmeg, cloves, and vanilla, though the traders were sure to bring those. Not news, though chances were a bard would be traveling with the traders and would entertain the town for more than one afternoon telling stories.

"Indigo," Joey finally said. "And sugar." He paused, then added, "And horses. And more trained birds."

The silence from the others made Joey look down at his feet, dangling from the wall, wishing a hole would suddenly appear that he could slip into. He'd said something strange again, hadn't he?

Then Max burst into laughter. "Indigo. Of course! Why didn't I think of that?"

"I don't even know what that is," Bridgette added.

"It's a dye," Han Lee said. "It's very rare. Comes from plants that only grow in warm areas, not around here. It makes a beautiful blue cloth."

Joey threw Han Lee a grateful smile. "Mom said something about it this morning," he lied. He didn't know why he'd said *indigo*. It had just seemed right to him. He hadn't even known what it meant.

Of course, when the traders arrived, they had several cakes of very rare indigo that they'd found in one of the ancient places, preserved in glass jars.

Along with sugar, horses, and more trained birds.

"So you're the young man who predicted the indigo, eh?" came a voice from over Joey's shoulder.

Joey looked behind him and gulped.

The person addressing him was the bard who traveled with the traders. He'd touched magic frequently enough that his brown eyes were flaked with gold. His pale face looked human, though. He wore a regular work shirt, off-white with thin blue stripes, made with a simple collar and buttons. Over that, he wore a patchwork vest, made from scavenged materials, the brighter the better, it seemed.

Joey had walked into Lakeland with his mom so she could trade some of the herbs they grew out on the Blue Dragon farm. While she conducted her business, Joey had wandered away from the town square and gone to look at the new roof being put on the Manenor family's house, about a block away.

Joey shrugged at the bard's statement. He hadn't meant to. He really tried to fit in, to stay human.

However, he knew that some townsfolk were already predicting that he'd turn into a magician. Mom and Da watched him sometimes. It made him mad, particularly on nights when the *myst* howled outside the farmhouse. He wasn't about to spout horns or something!

And he'd kill himself if he started growing *wyrd*. He'd just never hurt his family that way.

"I'm Billy," the bard said, placing his pink palms together over his chest, then bowing his head. "Billy the bard. At your service."

They didn't shake hands, though Joey knew it wasn't really possible to spread magic that way. That wasn't how it worked. He just knew it. Still, people no longer touched strangers, not ever.

And this Billy was stranger than most. Already, Joey felt the hairs on the back of his neck standing up.

"I'm Joey," he said, repeating the gesture. What did this bard want? What else had he heard? How soon could Joey go back to his mom?

"Magicians come in all shapes and sizes. In powers great and small," Billy said, peering closely at Joey. "I've known magicians who could shake mountains. Or divert a flooding river and thereby save a town. But I've never heard of a magician who could foresee the future."

"I can't tell the future," Joey said. "And I'm not a magician. I don't work magic. I don't call it to me. I don't try to use it. Stuff just…happens." It had all his life. He was more sensitive to magic and the *myst* than any of his friends, or even the adults, but he'd never cast a spell or felt compelled to make a charm.

He'd never wanted to *use* magic. It was just there. Like it was for everyone.

"Then the indigo was just a lucky guess?" Billy asked. "You were just thinking about what sorts of things the traders could be bringing and the word just popped into your head?"

"That's exactly what happened!" Joey said. Something was bothering though, something that gnawed at the back of his head, telling him that that *wasn't* exactly what had happened, but he ignored that little voice.

"No, no, no, my boy, you and I know there's no such thing as that kind of coincidence," Billy said, shaking his head.

"But I didn't use magic," Joey said. He never had. He didn't want to use magic. Didn't want to slice up his soul.

Joey wanted to get married someday. Maybe to Han Lee. They could have kids, sons and daughters, who would help him in the fields, just like he'd helped Da all his life. And they'd stay out on the Blue Dragon farm. Grow old together as the seasons changed.

"There's no shame in working magic, lad," the bard assured Joey. "I'm not ashamed. I help people. I do."

"That's good," Joey said. He stopped himself from taking a step back from this strange bard, despite the unease he felt.

All magicians were strange. Normal people could tell. There was just something about a magician, something that made people uneasy.

At least no one had ever told Joey that he made them uneasy.

Billy took a step closer. "Though there are many fates that flow away from every decision we ever make, I think your life has narrowed," he predicted, looking Joey up and down. "I don't think you'll be able to walk easily away from this one. I think your path is being set. Whether you want to walk along it or not."

Were his eyes glowing? What did he see?

"I'll make my own path," Joey said stubbornly. He'd refused to use magic so far. He could resist doing it forever, if it meant being able to stay with his family and friends.

Being able to stay *normal.*

"You may not have a choice to stay as you are," Billy said. "Every town is going to need all the magicians they can grow."

Was he reading Joey's mind? Did he know how much Joey desired to remain the same?

"It's some of the news we carry. The *myst* is spreading. Growing stronger," Billy added, dropping his voice.

Joey nodded. He could see that here in Lakeland. Any field that wasn't protected with charms or salt, any trees that didn't have sachets hanging in them, would get taken. The *myst* hemmed Lakeland in on all sides now. He remembered when there were more open places where he could play, more nights quiet and still.

"There's a town, not too far from here, that's gone now. Trees full of deadly creatures grown up, overnight, where there used to be fields and houses," Billy told him.

"So they weren't careful enough," Joey said, though it was something he knew the adults were worried about, that the *myst* might suddenly try to overwhelm them.

"Salt tribes, too, are having difficulties," Billy continued, as if Joey hadn't said anything. "Normally, *myst* and sand don't mix. But the *myst* has been seen on the shore, now."

Joey opened his mouth, then closed it again. If they couldn't get salt, how would they protect their fields and houses?

"We need to fight the *myst*," the bard said. "You and me. All of us. Or humankind will be wiped out."

"How?" Joey asked. "How can you fight something that's like…fog?" The *myst* was spread out everywhere. Not just here in Lakeland on the west coast and across what had been the United States, but all over the world, as far as anyone knew. Humans couldn't burn it or trap it or poison it. Only magic would stop it, the magic of the witches or The Fanged One or Beagle Boy. Not human magic.

"I don't know," Billy said. He leaned forward, close enough that Joey could smell sour cheese and beer on his breath. "That's why I'm going to see the oracle."

"The oracle?" Joey said. He'd never heard of an oracle. No one could tell the future, not even him, despite what people might think.

"The Great Inland Sea, eh?" the bard said. "She absorbed all the knowledge of the city of Seattle. And she's now become quite a philosopher. She'll know how to fight the *myst*, if anyone does."

"If she knew how to fight the *myst*, wouldn't she have told someone before now?" Joey asked. That kind of knowledge shouldn't be kept secret. Everyone should know.

Billy shrugged. "She only sometimes answers questions. But she'll listen to me," Billy assured Joey. "I've got songs to sing to her, lyrics she's never heard before. Poems to court her with." Billy gave Joey an exaggerated wink. "Maybe she'll want to be my bride. And not drown me like the others."

People had died going to see her? Joey shivered. "Well, good luck," he said. He needed to get back to the marketplace. Mom would probably be finished with her trades and gossip by now.

"You could come with us," Billy called after Joey had turned to go. "Join our merry troop. Fight the good fight."

"I can't," Joey said. "I need to stay here. Work on the farm. Help my family."

"The greatest help for your family will be defeating the *myst*," Billy told him.

Joey hurried away. He knew that—everyone knew that. The *myst* was growing stronger. Maybe not every day, but every year. More places were lost. It took more to defend their fields and houses.

More people went *wyrd*, maddened by the *myst* and magic and unable to handle it anymore.

But it wasn't Joey's job. He needed to be here, with his family and their fields.

Though if he did go to the Great Inland Sea to ask a question, it wouldn't be how to defeat the *myst*.

He'd ask her about how to hatch the blue-dragon-egg rocks.

# Five

Riffen floated away from the house, the night winds tugging at her dandelion skirt. She continued to sing her spring song, "La-de-de, la-de-da, la-de-dum" as she twirled through the air. She'd whispered her news through the cracks, telling of the pacts between Ocean and *myst* breaking, of the funny traders who would be coming to the town soon, of yet another magician who had lost her soul to magic and wouldn't be coming back to Lakeland.

Did the people in the house hear her news? She sang it to them every night, like about the traders who had just come to town and the indigo they carried. However, she was just the spring witch. It was the winter witch who was the closest to the family who hid behind the tall eves.

Riffen remembered, or rather, she had the memories from her sisters, of the boys and girls who would come to the window whenever she called.

No one had come for her, though. Not for the entire season.

Still, she floated down, closer to the house, brushing her fingertips across the lovely flowers planted there. They did remember and honor her, at least, and planted the flowers she liked in safe places, so their colors and fragrance would fuel her, like the sparse sunlight.

Then she floated up, past the garden where wonderful herbs grew, to the tower the family had built.

With the *myst* encroaching on all sides, it was lovely to have a safe place to rest. Riffen landed at the very top of the tower, sitting on the platform there. She couldn't help but sing more of her spring song, "De-de-la-la, da-da-la-la, dum-dum-dum."

A bird chirped once from nearby. Was it a real, old-fashioned bird? Or yet another spy for the *myst*? She should remember to tell the family about the birds someday. That they should put up birdhouses with mirrors on them. The real birds wouldn't notice the mirrors, and would appreciate having a safe home as well. The spies wouldn't use them.

Some of the traders knew this secret. She wondered who had told them. There were so many small gods now—creatures like her that the humans prayed to, like the cat-woman and the dog-boy. Riffen remembered—or carried memories from her sisters of what they'd been like before they'd become small gods.

But really, there was only so much she could do to hold back the *myst*. She built traps for it, gateways and tunnels made of spring sunlight and winds that held back the *myst*. But she couldn't tunnel all the way through the forests. The cat-girl with the tattooed fangs could blow her smoke and drive the *myst* away, but only for a while. The dog-boy built webs that trapped the *myst*, but he couldn't cover the forests either.

The humans needed more than just them, more than just what the small gods could offer.

And soon. The *myst* had yet to find its champion. Once it did, its attack would be horribly swift and sure.

And mankind would be no more.

## Six

Erin woke up someplace new. Again. Tree branches spread out above her, not the ceiling she'd fallen asleep watching. Crickets hummed nearby. Off in the distance, fake-birds called, offering fake cheer. The sun had just come up—she could feel its newness in the air.

At least the sky was clear. Erin hated going from someplace sunny to someplace rainy, or worse, snowy. She pushed herself up, taking stock.

She wore the same clothes—the hideously scratchy brown dress, that awful rope around her waist, rope sandals tied to her feet. She reached up and smiled when she touched her hair. It was the only thing that she could claim as hers anymore, the odd way her hair hung down on one side and not on the other.

Erin had never tried to remove her outfit. She'd always assumed that whatever had taken her had dressed her in such an ugly dress for a reason. It probably protected her from the *myst*.

When she'd had enough of this life, she could always go running naked through the woods. Whatever had saved her before would probably let her go.

Maybe.

At least the magician last night—Abraham?—had fed her. Most didn't. They were too far gone down the path of magic and barely ate themselves. They wouldn't think to feed a visitor.

Erin sighed and pushed herself up. She knew she'd have at least a day in this new place. It was rare that she'd have two. It was early in the morning yet. She'd have to pick a direction and start walking.

If she was lucky, she'd run into kids before she saw any adults—kids who wouldn't ask as many questions about who she was or where she'd come from.

Kids who would gladly tell her about any magicians living nearby.

Erin didn't know who had put her on this path, who moved her around like some life-size doll every day or so, dropping her someplace new almost every morning. She'd been all over what had once been called the Americas—North, South, and United. Only a couple of times had she been to places where no one looked like her, and no one spoke any English.

Those had been scary times, when she'd been afraid the locals would just decide she was *wyrd* and kill her.

Was it a small god moving her around so? She didn't think so. They were all dedicated to a particular area. Every town or village she'd visited had their own small gods, generally more than one, though never more than five.

Erin hadn't been told by whoever was doing this to her to go talk to magicians every time she was put down. She'd decided to do that all on her own. She had no idea why she was traveling as she did, what she was supposed to be learning or doing.

But whatever power was moving her didn't seem to mind her finding magicians, talking to them, asking them about magic.

She was certain she just had to find the one, the *right* one, who could teach her how to get home.

# Seven

Billy the bard couldn't believe how clear the morning was, how the sun shone down upon the waters of the Great Inland Sea, how it sparkled and shone. Tall green grasses grew on the shore and waved gently in the breeze. There was no end to the sea as it stretched north—the water ran all the way to the horizon.

To the west lay the hulking ruins of Seattle. Bare iron beams forced their way out of the salt marsh, arrogantly reaching toward the sky. Oh, what man had wrought!

Billy couldn't imagine living in such a warren. Even if the *myst* didn't hem in the city, it still felt closed in to him, those towers dominating the sky, making him feel puny.

The sea didn't make him feel that way. She brought poetry to his soul, that majestic soaring of spirit.

Surely today the Oracle would answer him!

Billy knew the traders he'd traveled to the Great Inland Sea with wouldn't wait much longer—maybe a day, maybe two—before they headed back south along the trade routes, picking up what they thought would be useful in one town to trade in the next.

This group even spent time and magical resources scrounging and scavenging in the larger, abandoned cities, finding things to sell, like the indigo. But the cities were getting more dangerous, even for the most powerful of mages.

The traders had already made twice the profit this year compared to the previous year. It was the only reason why they'd agreed to come to the Great Inland Sea, for Billy to ask his questions of the Oracle.

Plus, maybe there would be towns here they could trade with. No one had been this far north for a decade or more. Towns shifted, dissolved or sprang up, all the time. None were known to exist up here—but maybe they could find some.

And besides. If Billy could get the Oracle to answer his questions about the *myst,* they could be rich beyond their wildest dreams. People would trade all of their crops for a way to beat the *myst.* For some method to drive it back and away.

To live freely, without the constant fear and dread the *myst* rained down on them.

The primary magician for the group, Daneen, joined Billy as he looked out over the sea.

"Pretty day," she said, her golden eyes glowing brightly. "Too pretty."

Billy looked around. He couldn't see as well as she could—none of them could—but she was also prone to pessimism.

There wasn't anything there that set off any warnings for him. No *myst* dared come close to the sea—it hung back in the city of Seattle, in the vast trees and hills to the north and east of the city. No birds hung in the sky. Even the seagulls kept a decent distance away, though Billy had always thought seagulls were friendly creatures.

"Why do you think the *myst* and the water fight?" Billy asked.

Daneen shrugged. "They both want the same space. Only one can win." She turned her baleful stare at him. "Make sure it's the one who favors us."

Billy wasn't sure what Daneen meant. Water didn't want to overwhelm the land. And the *myst* couldn't live in the water. It made more sense for them to agree to inhabit different areas.

Or was she talking about something more metaphorical, like the space between them, where man lived and worshipped?

It didn't matter. Today was sure to be the day.

"Only one more day," Daneen warned as Billy nodded to her, preparing to get closer to the water.

Billy hesitated, then nodded again. One more day to prove himself to the sea. To persuade the Oracle to talk with him and answer his questions.

It was possible that she didn't know the answer, didn't know how to defeat the *myst*, as that one boy—Joshua? Joseph?—had proclaimed.

Billy was certain she knew the answer. The Great Inland Sea had absorbed all the mysteries of the ancients. Surely she talked with Ocean as well. Maybe there were other lands, other manmade civilizations that had already defeated the *myst*.

Perhaps Billy wasn't asking the question right. He went through his script, adjusting his prayers, rephrasing things yet again.

Today, his performance for the Great Inland Sea would be perfect. She would reply.

He just knew it.

"But soft, what sparkling creature through yonder window comes? Is it the sun? No, it is a maid far more lovely than that. It is my love, the one and only, incomparable beauty of the West. The Sea, ever, to the Sea."

Billy knew the words were only similar to the original. He'd always considered that his greatest talent, to be able to judge an audience and adjust his performance, to give them what they needed. One needn't be a stickler for reproducing the ancient's works. You had to give audiences what they wanted, instead.

The Great Inland Sea was the toughest audience he'd ever played for. Still, he thought he was getting somewhere with her.

"Let your face show in yonder window. Bless me with your glorious gaze. Let me grow in your light, always turning toward you, like the flowers follow the sun," Billy continued. "You shine so much brightly than any star in the sky, who have all turned green with envy at your brilliance."

Was that wave a bit higher than the others? There wasn't any wind, but the water seemed more agitated than it had been earlier. Choppier.

He was making progress.

"What we need is to communicate," Billy said, switching roles. "Not just as boy and girl. Man and woman. Venus and Mars. But you and me. Mano-a-sea-o. There are things I've seen, far from here, that you, the great repository of knowledge, would like to know. While I beg of you, *beg* of you, I would like to share your knowledge too."

Yes, the waves were definitely more choppy now. No wind blew from the sea, but Billy still felt as though every word was being whipped away from him and carried over the water.

He just had to convince the Great Inland Sea that she wanted to reply as well.

"O great font of knowledge. This is Man, the only, calling. We have need of your wisdom. Of your guidance. Let us talk of the great ships that once traversed your waters, of your sister seas, of secrets protected with sealing wax, of the growth of cabbages and the fall of kings."

Water suddenly lapped at Billy's feet. The sea had risen so quickly! He hadn't even noticed it. Or had she blinded his eyes so she could approach him without remark?

"Thank you for bathing my feet in your greatness," Billy said smoothly. He didn't try to move out of the way.

A larger wave struck his legs, pushing him back.

But no words came yet.

"Please, I implore you," Billy said. He fell to his knees. The cold of the water made him gasp. He'd expected the Great Inland Sea to be more warm. "We need your help. If man is to survive. How do we defeat the *myst?*"

He felt very gauche just asking the question out loud, without more poetry. But he also had the feeling his time was short. The waves had a definite impatient quality to them.

Had he misjudged his audience? Did the Great Inland Sea need more directness, less poetry?

*You can't.* The answer wasn't in direct words, but the feeling was undeniable.

"So man is destined to lose?" Billy shouted, his hands clenching into claws as hope was torn from him. How could this be? Man had survived for almost two centuries since the rifts, since the bombs had opened the world to the *myst.*

*Not necessarily.*

That surprised Billy. Maybe there was a chance. He'd felt so bereft before! Was that Her doing? He gasped and tried to open his eyes wider, but the green, oh, the lovely green was washing over him.

"Then how?" Billy asked, struggling to stay on his knees and not just lie down, belly deep, in the muck and mud of the shore. "How do we win?"

*Wrong question.*

A great wave surged up before Billy, at least the size of a house. In it, Billy saw reflections of the greatest ancients, of Venus herself carried over the waves, Athena hunting for answers, and Hera shaking the keys of the household at him. Of the great bard himself, scribbling and throwing away page after page, of a great chapel with ceilings covered in murals, of beautiful stone buildings with ethereal stained glass windows that glowed with their own light.

*The questions should be, how do you* survive.

The brightest light shone into Billy's eyes as he tried to breathe but only sucked more water into his lungs, the wave collapsing down on him, or had it already collapsed before she'd spoken a single word?

*So you lose,* the Oracle informed Billy as she took him down, dragging him under the water. She peeled his skin away from him, peeled his knowledge and his poetry and his performances off, absorbing all of it, all of *him*, until there was no more.

Then the waters smoothed out and the sea became a great seeing-glass again, perfectly reflecting the sky above it as well as everything else she saw.

She let the others go, to bear witness to her strength. To maybe bring someone she would enjoy playing the question-and-answer game with.

And possibly to spread the word, so that someone, someday, would come and ask the right questions.

# Eight

Joey followed the curve of the strip of field as it meandered. On his left ran a low rock wall that almost rose to his waist, made out of rejects, stones that weren't quite right for the tower, that weren't blue-dragon-egg rocks. On his right ran a boxwood hedge, about the same height, that he and the others kept well trimmed and weeded. Raspberry vines—maybe *myst*-controlled, maybe not—had tried sprouting through the boxwood leaves that spring and had had to be pulled out.

While it was possible to keep berry vines tame and safe, it took time and effort that Joey and his family didn't want to put in, not in the middle of the wheat field.

But the wheat was doing well that year. They'd already put in a second crop. If the rains came, and if the sun came, and if the *myst* didn't try to take over the fields, they should have more than enough to make it through the winter.

At only sixteen, Joey feared a winter without enough wheat as much as the adults.

Overhead the sun shone down strong. Joey sweated in his long pants and boots and long-sleeved shirt, but he couldn't go out with less, like some of the men did when they weren't working the fields. Da had always said it was easier to repair cloth than skin, and you never knew what could get you walking outside.

Joey stopped suddenly, lifting his head. Something had changed. Though he might not want to be so sensitive to magic, he knew it helped, helped keep him alive, helped warn the others when something came up.

Was it the birds? He'd seen seagulls flying earlier, two apparently chasing the other one, circling and wheeling through the air. He didn't know which of them to root for—his magic sense didn't expand that far. They perched now in the woods at the edge of the fields, calling loudly to each other. There weren't any other birds above him, not as far as he could see in the clear sky.

Joey lifted his foot to take another step, then looked down.

There, between the rows of plants, lay the small body of a chickadee.

Joey squatted down to get a better look. The bird panted, still alive, though ants were already crawling on it. Small pinpoints of blood covered its breast, and when Joey rocked it to the side to see its back, found much more blood there. It chirped weakly at him.

This wasn't one of the spy birds, who acted in consort with the *myst*, who stripped fields bare or even attacked people who were walking alone, without protection. This was one of the innocent ones, the friendly birds, who still helped and ate insects and sang out warnings about the demon birds and the *myst*.

Joey wasn't surprised that it had been attacked.

Intense curiosity filled Joey. Could he save it? That would mean touching magic. Did he want to? Just for this creature? He wanted to know, suddenly, what magic might feel like.

Joey wasn't sure he could avoid magic, no matter how much he might want to. He was sensitive to it. And Lakeland needed magicians.

How did a magician touch magic, anyway? Joey had never done it consciously before. He stood up and looked out, across the field, to the trees that hemmed in the edges. Slight traces of *myst* hung from the branches, pale and deadly.

How could Joey work with *that?* He'd heard the *myst* howl and scream at night. He'd felt it press against him like a humid summer day when the air was so wet, when he'd passed too near. It was *evil.* Deadly.

Somehow, though, magicians found that balance between drawing power out of the *myst* and yet not drawing too much, staying (mostly) themselves and not turning *wyrd.*

Joey just wanted to help the little bird. Either heal it of its wounds, or wring its neck so it wouldn't suffer.

When Joey looked back from the trees he didn't scream, but he did take a quick step back.

Someone was standing there, in front of him. How had she gotten there? Who was she? He didn't recognize her.

And he knew all the magicians near Lakeland.

"You're doing it wrong," she told him. Her golden eyes were deep set under a bulging brow. Light brown hair covered her face, while darker brown hair flowed down her back, long and sleek. Her ears had migrated to the top of her head and looked more like dog ears. She wore old clothes from the abandoned places—a shimmering white blouse that didn't hide her breasts, jeans, and pointed leather boots.

"Who are you?" Joey asked. He felt ashamed that she'd found him trying magic for the first time. She was obviously a strong magician. He made himself look at her, though there was just something *wrong* about her. Cascades of goose bumps went down his spine. She wasn't evil, not like the *myst*. But she wasn't right, either. Maybe it was because of her alien features, though Joey felt it went further, something bone deep.

"Lisel," she said, amused. "And you don't *invite* the *myst* in. That way lies madness. You must find where the *myst* and the magic already lie, deep inside you."

"But there's no magic inside me!" Joey replied. Was there? He'd never felt it.

"There's a great well of magic inside you," Lisel told him. "More than most. It's why you're so sensitive to it. Like follows like."

"How do I find it?" Joey asked, curious despite his general aversion to all things magical.

Lisel shrugged. "Can't teach you that. It's different for each person. I know one magician who thinks of it as a layer of skin, just under his own. Another described a core of quicksilver running through him, bright and malleable. Me—I found the wolf."

Her features melted and her face transformed. In moments, she had the head of a wolf, a great slobbering beast with sharp teeth. However, her eyes were still golden. Not human, but not animal either.

They just looked wrong. Monstrous. Like a creature from nightmares carried at night on the wind from the *myst*.

Joey took another step back, his hand going to the knife he always wore on his belt. She wasn't about to attack him, was she?

Lisel bent forward quickly. She snatched up the injured bird on the ground, grabbed it by the tail with her mouth, then tossed it up in the air. It chirped one last time before it fell into Lisel's great open mouth. She swallowed it whole.

Joey shivered in the bright sunlight. Magicians were supposed to be their allies. Had this one gone *wyrd?*

Lisel laughed, a strange barking sound coming from a wolf's head. The words she spoke didn't come from her mouth—they were just said, out loud, so Joey could hear them. "You'll learn," she said. She sounded deeply satisfied. "Or else."

Then she vanished, leaving Joey alone.

What had just happened? Was she some sort of traveling magician? None of the other magicians he knew could just vanish like that. Or was she a small god? Except that the gods didn't talk with people. Not really.

He knelt down, looking where the bird's body had lain. There was blood still on the dirt. Ants. And the smell of sweet incense. It reminded him of the smoke The Fanged One blew.

Joey shivered again, then quickly left the fields.

He wasn't ever going to be like that. No matter how sensitive he was to magic.

# Nine

The Whiskered One rapidly swung from one branch to the next, racing to the northern edge of his jungle, closest to the town of Tulum in the former Mexican Yucatan. Normally, he'd enjoy stretching his limbs as he swung from tree to tree, his long white moustache flowing freely, his tail rising and falling, keeping him balanced. Now, though, it was a mighty race.

He'd worked hard to keep the *myst* at bay, keep his jungle mostly free of its insidious fog. His people lived so close to the trees and often ventured under their branches. They needed the medicines and fruits the jungle provided for them, as well as the resin they collected for the incense they burned to honor him.

But now, The Whiskered One had learned of another attack by the *myst*. And it was happening so soon after the last one! On the other edge of the jungle, almost directly opposite to where the *myst* last attacked.

It was almost as if the *myst* was testing him.

If he failed to keep the *myst* at bay, his people would lose faith in him. Stop visiting him. Stop praying to him and praising his dark fur, his long white whiskers. Stop burning incense for him—the sweet copal that they'd burned for their ancestors.

The blight was easy to spot—a white fog, growing like a poisonous fungus, at the tops of the trees. But it was no ordinary fog, no morning mist caught among the branches.

The Whiskered One flung himself into battle. He had extra hands that his tamarin ancestors hadn't—Man hands, with proper thumbs, protruding from his center—that he used along with his top hands to rapidly braid vines, creating a powerful whip. He flicked it through the air, once, twice, the angry *snap* reflecting his own rage.

*Back*, he commanded. His whip cut into the leading edge of the *myst* threatening to drape itself over the trees, *his* trees.

The *myst* pulled back into itself, its edges shredded.

The Whiskered One struck with his whip again and again, seeking out every tiny tendril the *myst* put forth. He couldn't show any mercy, couldn't rest until it was driven away.

The *myst* gathered itself up into a stubborn ball, as if daring The Whiskered One to attack it.

But he knew better. That ball was actually a writhing mass of snakes. If he hit it with just his whip, it would explode, and the *myst* would go everywhere. He might never be able to clean it up, disperse every tiny worm that crawled on the underside of the leaves.

He'd learned that lesson the hard way.

Instead, The Whiskered One pulled back and braided another whip. Then a third, a fourth, and more. Until he could weave them together in a net.

However, the *myst* knew this trick too. It, too, had learned. The ball grew multiple snake heads, sleek and quick, ready to slip through the holes in the net The Whiskered One threw at it.

The Whiskered One paused again, contemplating his old enemy. The seductive, hidden thoughts came unbidden. *Just a few trees. That's all you have to lose. Then we'll leave you alone. Let you rest.*

The Whiskered One knew the *myst* lied. It would never be satisfied with just a few trees. It didn't want just his jungle—no, it planned to take over all the land, then cover Ocean and her Sisters with clouds and fog, so that she would die off as well.

It was more arrogant than Man, thinking of itself as the only important being on earth, needing to spread itself everywhere.

Still, The Whiskered One readied two more whips. These were braided with special ends, flayed cattails instead of a single, focused point.

The Man hands in the center of The Whiskered One held the special whips at the ready, while his lower hands/feet held the net. His upper hands kept him steady on the tree branch, ready to swing in whatever direction the enemy went.

The old feeling of despair came over The Whiskered One. *You'll never win. There aren't enough of the small gods. You'll fail, and so will Man.*

The Whiskered One threw his net over the writhing ball of *myst* anyway, then started destroying each snake as it slithered out. His arms rose and fell in a syncopated manner, the whips snapping, the *myst* hissing. He knew the battle would be long and epic.

If any of his people were there to witness it, they would write poems about it. Add to their songs of praise.

But that wasn't why The Whiskered One fought. He fought because it was the right thing to do, the only thing he could do. It was why he'd been born, after all, after the bombs and the rifts, coming awake in the Jungle to guide the few humans who'd remained there.

His people had grown. Thrived.

He would see them live on.

He would drive *myst* away from this side of the jungle today, cleansed from the trees. The Whiskered One was more determined than ever to fight, despite the despair and bleakness approaching. He'd fight until he could no longer move, no longer had breath in him.

He might not win, not in the end. Not he or the Iguana Girl or any of the other small gods who'd risen to fight the *myst*.

But that was no reason to stop.

# Ten

Ima crouched beneath a flea-infested blanket at the back of the barn. God, she *hated* her dad. Ever since Mom had died—and had the *myst* really gotten her? Or had he killed her?—he'd turned his attention toward her.

It hadn't been bad, at first. Just watching her. And holding her hand. And telling her that she was now the woman of the house, though she was only fourteen.

But now…Ima shuddered and tried to close her ripped blouse over her chest. God, how could he have tried to *do* those things to her? She'd been able to stop him by calling him "Daddy" and reminding him that she was his little girl.

Would it be enough the next time he decided he wanted her like that?

Was there anyone in town that she could tell? Would anyone believe her? Would the Town Elders protect her?

She'd been pretty obnoxious after her mom had died. She was willing to admit that. Maybe before then, as well. Wearing men's pants instead of women's dresses, like they had in the days of the ancients. She'd seen pictures, they all had.

But the Elders weren't right, either, insisting that the women wear dresses all the time and stay at home, never venturing outside.

Ima *hated* being stuck inside all the time. Plus, she was strong. She could help in the fields. She knew other girls did, in other towns. The traders had talked about them, before the Elders decided that the traders were no longer welcome.

Now, Ima had gotten her wish. Her dad had forced her outside after she'd refused him, dragging her by her hair, then throwing her into the dark space of the unprotected barn.

"You can play with your horsies and your dolls here instead of being a grownup," he'd sneered as he'd locked the barn door.

She hated him. So much. Maybe she could find a way to the next town in the morning. Other kids had run away. Begged the traders to take them away. Before the Elders tracked them down and sacrificed them to the ancient gods.

If she survived the night.

A soft light suddenly started glowing in the far corner of the barn.

"Stay away!" Ima cried.

God, she would be a good girl. Do what he wanted. She didn't want the *myst* to get her.

A sense of curiosity flowed over her.

Was that the *myst* talking to her? Did it want to know why she was there? Or why she didn't want to go with the *myst?*

The feeling of curiosity intensified.

Ima decided it wanted to know why she was there.

She could tell, somehow, that words wouldn't work. The *myst* dealt with emotions. So she thought about her dad, what he'd tried to do to her, how much she hated him.

She felt the hate blossom under her skin as if a fire had abruptly lit up her belly.

*Hate.* The *myst* understood hate. That was part of its nature, to hate, to be hated.

Ima started feeling a sense of kinship with it. The *myst* encouraged the hatred in her, mingled with another feeling. A new thing that pushed Ima beyond fear.

The sense of getting even. Of *revenge.*

Though the *myst* still didn't speak in words, Ima would practically hear it.

*Do you want to get revenge on the one who left you in here? Left you to us? Like he did your poor mother?*

Ima shivered. She'd learned early, watching her mom bargain with the tradesmen who came to the door every day, that there was always a cost for things, a bargain to be made.

She wanted revenge. Her hands turned to claws, ready to scratch her dad's eyes out at the thought of it. But she didn't want to die.

*Live,* the *myst* promised her. *Stronger. Better.*

A feeling of warm strength flowed over Ima. Her bruised arms suddenly healed. She couldn't instantly grow back the hair that her dad had yanked out of her head, but those places on her scalp stopped throbbing. Even her jaw popped back into place, from where he'd dislocated it, hitting her with his fist.

She felt healthy. Well fed. Capable.

Better than she had since her mom had died.

"And what do you want from me?" Ima asked out loud while she tried to get across the sense of trade, of *bargain* to the *myst.*

Her arms lifted and then gently lowered again, her hands tingling.

The *myst* needed her hands. It needed her to do something. Something physical that it couldn't manifest and do.

The door to the barn opened. No one stood there. But she was free.

Free to go kill her dad. The *myst* would help.

Then all she had to do was help the *myst.* Just this once. And then she'd be free.

Did the *myst* lie?

Did it matter?

Ima knew that the price was either do this for the *myst,* or die.

She chose to live.

# Eleven

Manuel looked up from his desk. The three black slates that took up the top of it were full of scratched chalk marks and scribbled notes—tallied workers for the week.

Saul stood just inside the door to his hut, looking shamefaced. He'd be scuffing his toes along the dirt floor next, and sighing.

"Don't tell me," Manuel said sourly, putting down his piece of chalk and vainly wiping his hands against each other, trying to clear away the dust. "There's another one."

"Yes, yes, there iz," Saul said, nodding his head vigorously.

"We don't have space," Manuel growled. The bunk houses were already overcrowded. They could barely feed the crowd that they had. Manuel and his team had strategy meetings every week now, trying to figure out the increasingly complicated logistics.

But people kept showing up. Mostly men, some women, who'd been drawn to the northern side of Mount Rainier.

Damned mountain kept calling them, too. People would fight *myst* and who knew what else to get there, to the camp, to New Mountain Town. They came from all over what had been the Americas, not just up and down the west coast. They weren't about to leave, either. Not until they got their fill of worship, or whatever the hell the mountain wanted from them before it let them go.

No one had made Manuel the chief of New Mountain Town. He'd kind of appointed himself, many years before.

Manuel had grown up in the shadow of Mount Rainier. Every year, a group of young men and women would make the pilgrimage to the base of the mountain, to show their skill against the *myst* and the creatures in the forest as well as their bravery.

He'd heard about the pilgrims, the ones the mountain had called to it. They sometimes passed through his village on the way to the mountain. The villagers referred to them as the crazy ones, though they weren't *wyrd* and hurtful.

Seeing the pilgrim camp for the first time had shocked the young people in his group.

It had pissed Manuel off. People didn't have to live that way, with shacks that barely had walls, no sewers, and everyone starving. Why hadn't his village done anything to help them?

He'd tried to talk with his fellow travelers, but they didn't want anything to do with the pilgrims.

But Manuel wasn't scared of them. Nor was he afraid that staying too close to the mountain may drive him either crazy or *wyrd*.

He'd started organizing pilgrims that afternoon to dig latrines, the ones who could tear their gaze away from the hypnotic way the clouds rolled over the face of the mountain, covering Him then revealing Him, again and again.

Though the rest of his troop left, Manuel stayed behind, getting the worshippers organized, coaxing them into building New Mountain Town.

Which kept growing until Manuel wasn't really sure what he was going to do with close to two thousand souls.

"All right. All right," Manuel said, pushing himself up from the desk. He and his team rotated the duties of greeting the newcomers. They'd found it easier to ease the new pilgrims into the rest of New Mountain Town if someone personally went and greeted them, showed them around, kept drawing their attention from the mountain to the streets and latrines and kitchens.

They had to make it clear from the very start that the pilgrim was only welcome to stay if they'd contribute.

Saul stayed where he was standing, not bowing and leaving. In many ways, Saul treated Manuel like he was part of the mountain, worthy of worship.

"Yes?" Manuel asked.

"Boss…thees one. He's different," Saul said.

"How different?" Manuel asked, worried. They hadn't had many of the *wyrd* make it all the way to New Mountain Town—most perished in the nearby woods, taken by the creatures of *myst* there.

Saul shrugged. "He's not all there. Simple."

Manuel blinked, surprised. How could someone *simple* make it through the woods, survive the monsters there, and get past the *myst*, alive? Maybe he was merely more distracted than the usual pilgrim. "Thank you for bringing this to my attention," Manuel said, bowing his head to Saul.

Normally, that would make Saul grin and bounce and obnoxiously hold his "superior" status over the others for a week. But this time, Saul still looked pensive. "Be careful, boss." Then he shuffled his feet again and left.

Manuel pulled his broad black hat off the shelf next to the door, creasing the brim. It had been salvaged from one of the nearby towns, made of thick black leather that kept the sun and rain off. One of the magicians that passed through the town with the traders had made the leather seem like new.

Manuel knew that in the stories of the ancients, the bad guys wore black hats.

He hoped that when people got around to telling his story, they'd describe him as a good guy.

Manuel walked directly to the area they kept for newcomers. It had a wooden roof to keep the rains off, and a great view of the mountain. Between the town and the mountain were several fields. Manuel and the others generally walked the newcomers through the fields, getting them to understand that they were welcome if they didn't just stare at the mountain, but also worked.

Most figured it out quickly. The few that didn't, left quickly, never to be heard from again.

The newcomer stood under the roof, gazing at the mountain. He was tall—six foot five, at least, with an extra inch added by his curly hair, dark brown and shot through with gray. He had a young face, but it was wrong.

Big blue-gray eyes bulged out of his head, and his jaw wasn't hinged right: It bit to the left, making it hard for his fat lips to smack together.

He had long, lanky arms and legs, with big hands and feet to match the rest of him. He wore little better than rags for a shirt, though his pants looked sturdy and new. He smelled of deep woods and sweat, and hadn't bathed in too long.

"Howdy," Manuel said, coming up slowly. He didn't want to startle the big guy.

"Hi," the guy said, turning to face Manuel and bobbing his head up and down, like it was on a spring.

Manuel could understand why Saul had called the guy simple. He sure did seem that way.

But was it real? Or was it just an act?

"I'm Manuel," he said as way of introduction.

"I'm Carl," the guy said. He made an abortive move with his hand, as if he was going to shake or something, then stuck both hands behind his back and looked shamed, like a boy caught with his hand in the cookie jar.

"It's all right, Carl," Manuel said, keeping his distance. "So what brings you to New Mountain Town?"

Carl shrugged. "I heard there was work. And men. Here."

Manuel rocked back on his heels. No one just came to New Mountain Town, particularly not to work. They were all drawn by the mountain. There was plenty of work to be had everywhere. Every town and village that Manuel had ever heard about could always use more farm hands. Particularly someone as big—and potentially as strong—as Carl looked.

"Where'd you come from?" Manuel asked.

Carl looked down and away, up at the mountain, then back at Manuel. "Down the coast," he said. "Bad town."

Manuel knew Carl was lying about something. Was he not from down the coast? Or was the town not bad?

"Let's take a walk," Manuel suggested. It was what they always did.

"Okay," Carl said, making that same bobbing motion with his head.

The first field was all wheat. The rows were well broken up with old walls, clumps of well-trimmed trees, and small groves of blackberries. No one farmed in straight lines that the *myst* could run along.

"Have you farmed before?" Manuel asked, watching how Carl examined the wheat.

"Hauled wheat. Big bundles," Carl bragged, holding out his arms to show how much harvested wheat he could carry. "And picked apples. Until the bees came."

Carl shivered, and Manuel almost joined him. Like the birds, some types of bees were strange now. The yellow-jacket wasps in particular built huge hives that hung from a tall limb of a tree down to the ground, composed of off-white paper with strange markings on it.

One of the men had boasted that he'd taken a nest apart during the winter, when the bees were hibernating, unraveling pages and pages of maps.

But maps of where? Of what? No one knew.

"Can you dig?" Manuel asked when they reached the edge of the field and neared the first latrine.

Carl wrinkled his nose but gave his strange bobbing nod. "Yes. Carl strong. Dig deep holes."

On hearing that, Manuel would have been willing to bet that at one time, Carl had been welcomed wherever it was that Carl had been living, a member of his community. He'd done more than one task, more than one job. Why had they driven him out? Carl wouldn't have left on his own—simple or not, it was too dangerous to travel alone.

Instead of going toward the kitchens and communal dining areas, Manuel turned toward the worship platforms. They were a dozen wooden steps, each long enough for about twenty people to stand on, covered with canvas awnings to provide some protection from the sun and rain.

The best view of the mountain was found on the steps. Even when clouds obscured the mountain and it couldn't actually be seen, the faithful still congregated and watched, as if they could still see it.

Newcomers had to be looked after, or they'd stand there, in rapt awe for days, not moving until they fell over from hunger and dehydration.

Manuel watched Carl as they approached a small group of men and women stood in respectful silence, watching the mountain. He waved at the group, then realized they weren't looking at him, couldn't really even see him.

When they got to the foot of the steps, people automatically parted, letting Manuel through. He led Carl to the center of the first step, then turned to see the mountain.

It was pretty that afternoon. Clouds covered the top half of it, but the bottom half was clear.

No one lived on the mountain—it wouldn't accept Man anymore.

It didn't accept the *myst* either, however. The trees on the slopes of the mountain were bare, unshrouded. That afternoon, the way the light struck them, they looked a dusky blue, covered in shadows.

Carl looked at Manuel, then at the mountain, then back at Manuel. He mimicked the way his neighbors stood, with his hands folded in front of him, bobbing his head now and again.

The mountain really *hadn't* called Carl. He'd come on his own.

Something *really bad* must have happened in his town for them to drive him away.

After a few more minutes, Manuel led Carl away. They hadn't gone too far before Carl asked, "What were they doing?"

"They worship the mountain," Manuel explained as they headed toward the kitchens.

"Ah. It has no *myst*," Carl surmised.

"That's true," Manuel replied. He hesitated, then said, "Carl, I have to ask. What happened, in the bad town? Why did they drive you away?"

"You're very smart," Carl said. "I'm not. One of the other boys. Jim. He did something bad to Ellie. Then he blamed me. And Ellie—Ellie said yes, I had. But I wouldn't do something bad like that! Not to a girl!" He started smacking one fist into his other palm.

"Shh, shh, calm down, big guy," Manuel said. He glanced around quickly—at least two of the worshippers had stopped along the path to the , waiting. They'd come quickly if Manuel called. Though Manuel could handle himself, Carl *was* a big guy and those huge fists would hurt.

Carl gave Manuel a large, lopsided grin. "That's what Uncle Dick used to call me." His face grew dark again. "They burned down our house. Uncle Dick—his breath didn't work after that. He told me to come here."

Manuel nodded. That wasn't all the story, he knew. Was it enough of the crucial details?

It wasn't just because Carl was simple. There was something about him, something *off*, like a magician. Something that set Manuel's teeth on edge, just a little. Something that had made Saul wary of him as well.

But Manuel wasn't going to turn Carl away. Whether Carl would survive another trip through the woods was anyone's guess. "You can stay here for a while," Manuel said slowly.

"I can? I can?" Carl asked joyfully. "Thank you! Thank you!" His arms came forward again, then he held them back.

Manuel knew Carl had wanted to give him a hug. The family he'd grown up in had been demonstrative, that was for certain. That was probably a good sign.

At one point, Carl had quite possibly been loved. Despite how he put Manuel on edge, there was probably good in him, as well.

However, Manuel still needed to protect the rest of New Mountain Town as well. He held up his hand. "I want to make sure that you'll work out for the community," he warned.

Carl nodded vigorously. "I'll work. I'll work hard. There's no better worker than me."

They walked into the communal dining room. Bench after bench filled the big tent. A line formed on one end, snaking by the large pots set up in the middle. The rich scents of chicken broth, fresh unleavened bread, and weak beer filled the air.

"You can stay, but you'll stay with a team for now, all right?" Manuel said. He decided to put Carl with the most faithful of the newcomers, the ones the others watched all the time. He'd check back in after one week. See how Carl was doing.

He didn't want to turn Carl away. But if Carl turned *wyrd* or something, or if the others had too many problems with him, Manuel had no problem dumping his ass on the slope of the mountain—securely tied—and letting the mountain take care of him.

# Twelve

*Sorry, Uncle Dick,* Carl told the mountain as he stood on the platform with the others, watching The Mountain change. It had been cool and rainy all day. Carl had been grateful for the work—chopping wood—that kept him moving and warm.

Mists shrouded the trees on The Mountain's slope. Clouds crowned The Mountain, chased across His face, hid Him from view. However, despite the clouds, Carl still felt The Mountain. Knew it was waiting. Just like him.

He hadn't meant to lie about what had happened. But the lies came so much easier, now. He'd learned what to say to make people turn away from him. Not look closer.

Manuel had looked closer than most.

Carl didn't like him.

Manuel didn't understand why people came here.

It wasn't because The Mountain was hard to look away from, though it was, sometimes, even for Carl. The Mountain was *changing*, and He wanted people to know. When He had first awoken, He was slow, like Carl. But He was quickening, every day. Becoming something new.

Carl still waved and bobbed his head at Manuel, made himself smile and play stupid.

Not that Carl was smart. He knew there was something wrong with his head, something that made it not work like all the others.

But he had a strong back and knew how to work hard, so people were willing to put up with his slowness.

*Sorry, Ellie*, Carl added. He hadn't meant for Jim to hurt her. But Jim did things, lots of things, Carl didn't like. Like how he'd hurt Uncle Dick, whose breath never had worked right, not since the fire Carl had set as a boy.

Or had that been Jim as well?

Jim had told Carl to come to The Mountain. Had kept him safe under the trees, fought the *myst* and the creatures there for him.

The Mountain seemed to quiet Jim. He barely talked with Carl anymore, barely raised his voice, echoing inside Carl's head.

Making Carl *do* things, the things that Jim wanted to do.

Because of all his new friends in New Mountain Town, Carl didn't feel lonely without Jim. He wasn't relieved, because Jim was still there. Would always be there. Carl knew he couldn't just run away from Jim. They were too tangled, like the blackberry briars.

Was Jim *changing* too? Becoming something else while they waited? It seemed that way sometimes. Carl didn't know what Jim could become though. Wasn't he bad enough?

The people beside Carl groaned suddenly. Thick clouds started gathering between The Mountain and the town.

Unnatural clouds.

Clouds full of hidden *myst*.

Carl groaned too, and shook, suddenly afraid.

He hated the *myst*. It was what had first woken Jim, when Carl had been just a boy. It had spoken words to Jim, words that Carl didn't understand. Had made Jim strong, stronger than Carl, sometimes.

The *myst* was speaking to Jim now. Loud words. Hateful words.

Normally, The Mountain spoke to them. But now, the *myst* had stolen the voice of The Mountain, standing between The Mountain and the town. The *myst* used His voice to spread its filth.

Carl tried to look away, but he was caught—he couldn't turn his attention away from The Mountain.

The *myst* poured its words into Carl's skull now, its hatred, its anger.

Carl's fists clenched with rage. He gulped air, shaking. He tried to fight back. He *liked* New Mountain Town. He *liked* his friends here, his brothers.

Okay, so he didn't like working so hard, but he needed to keep his place here. He didn't hate Manuel. Didn't want to burn down the communal hall. Didn't want to rape Tesa or Mei Yan. Didn't want to turn the Littlefield Creek red with blood.,

The Mountain blew hard winds at the clouds.

The *myst* scattered.

Carl took a deep, shuddering breath as he found he could look away again.

The men beside him nodded, murmuring uneasily.

They'd been caught by the *myst* too. Did they all have a Jim inside, just waiting to get out?

But then The Mountain called Carl again, made him gaze upon His changes.

Soon. They would all be changing soon.

# Thirteen

Joey waited with everyone else in town, standing on the side of the road, looking out on the Nyguns' family field. The Fanged One would be coming soon to bless the field, so the town could begin the Planting Festival that they held every spring. Bright spring sunshine shone down on them, though more rain threatened on the horizon and kept all the breezes cool.

Tables already full of herbed scones, pretzels, and sourdough biscuits also stood on the road, ready to be carried into the field after The Fanged One had blessed it. The women traditionally used the last of the winter wheat harvest for the spring festival. Bowls of fresh greens and new clover also sat on the tables, the traditional first tastes of spring.

The drawing for the lucky family's field to be blessed had been held just the week before, early in the morning. Da hadn't put their name in the pot, as was Schuller family tradition.

The witches only ever came to the Schuller family fields, as far as anyone could tell. Decades before, the town had objected to them getting extra blessing from The Fanged One. So Joey's family never participated in the drawing, though they always came into town to celebrate with the lucky winners.

Max didn't wait beside Joey. Joey pretended not to notice. Max was far too interested in Linda these days. Joey knew they'd be getting married soon. About time too: They'd both be turning seventeen later that year.

More adults lived past their forties now, though very few, still. They lost their sensitivity to magic as they grew older, making it tough for them to survive. More women survived than men, but there were now at least a dozen fifty-year-olds in town, now.

Joey chose to stand close to Han Lee and her family. He still thought she was the prettiest girl in town. She smiled and waved at him, then turned away to talk with her sisters.

Joey knew he didn't have a chance with her. Despite how he vowed to *never* use magic, no one believed him. All of Lakeland believed he was going to become a magician someday. Everyone knew he was sensitive to it.

Some still thought he could foretell the future.

No girl would let him get close. Her family wouldn't either. Not if he was going to become a magician. He wouldn't be able to father children once he started touching magic. It changed people, too much. And if he had a wife, she wouldn't be able to stay with him, not once he became a magician and too strange.

So Joey stood alone on the side of the road, his family on one side, Han Lee's family on the other, watching the field. People chatted with their neighbors, speculated about the coming season, sent prayers to The Fanged One.

He'd never felt so alone.

Joey whipped his head to the side when The Fanged One arrived. He didn't see anyone standing on the far north end of the field. But he knew she was there.

People must have been paying attention to him, not watching the field, because everyone started pointing in the direction he stared in.

Just another indication that he was *different* than everyone else.

The Fanged One took her time materializing. A purple-tinged cloud slowly billowed out from where Joey was certain she stood, then dissipated, leaving The Fanged One behind.

More smoke billowed out from her great, tattooed fangs, that went from her upper jaw down past her chin to her white fur chest. Half a dozen tiny nipples peeked out of the fur, running down her torso. Around her waist hung a skirt made of green leaves that dropped down to her calves. Her feet were bare and mostly human, though covered in what looked like tough hide.

The Fanged One started making her way around the field, puffing out smoke from her fangs as she went. It was tinged purple as well, like the filigree engraved on her fangs. Winds that Joey couldn't feel carried the smoke across the field. It sank into the ground, blessing it, making the field more fertile. The Nyguns would have great crops that year.

It wasn't until The Fanged One drew closer that Joey could see her eyes, golden like a magician's, but different, too. They were wider, more animal, less human. She didn't pay any attention to the people standing in awed silence on the edge of the road. Her cat ears, on the top of her head, flicked back and forth.

Was she nervous? She should know that the people of Lakeland would never try to hurt her. Or was she just cautious?

Joey thought she looked tired. It was something in the way she moved, her limbs listless, her tail not batting at the air behind her.

He knew better than to say anything like that to anyone. They'd not only deny it but would shun him. The Fanged One was tireless in her battles with the *myst*.

But the *myst* continued to grow stronger, its area wider. How long could The Fanged One protect them?

When The Fanged One finished her circle, she stopped and looked back at them from the far side of the field.

Everyone put their hands together over their chests and bowed low to her. A chorus of "Thank you!" and "Bless you!" rang out.

The Fanged One repeated the gesture, bowing low to the townspeople. Then she vanished.

Joey let out a breath he hadn't known he'd been holding. He hadn't been afraid that The Fanged One wouldn't show up, not exactly. Or that she wouldn't bless the field they'd chosen, though that had happened once, years before Joey had been born. The father then murdered everyone in the family that night, before hanging himself, leaving the town to speculate if he'd actually turned *wyrd* and only The Fanged One had known.

But it still worried Joey that The Fanged One had looked so tired. It was like she still carried the clouds of winter with her, instead of the sunshine of spring.

There wasn't anyone he could ask about it, though. And he certainly wasn't about to approach Terri or the other magicians, though they might be the only ones who would know.

The *myst* was getting worse for everyone. Even for the small gods.

"Hi, Joey," Linda said as she came walking up to him.

Joey gulped down the last of the hard cider he'd been sipping. "Hi," he managed to croak out. At least he didn't spit it out all over her, or dribble it down his front. He stood next to the table now only partially full of pretzels, herbed scones, and unleavened garlic bread. Most of the families from town still gathered in the Nyguns' field. Kids held races along one side, while the adults stood in clusters, drinking and talking.

Linda was the type of girl that Joey just didn't get. She was as tall as he was, wore her long brown hair loose around her tan face, wore clothes that were homespun, yet she was as beautiful as the pictures of the perfect people that they'd find in old magazines and books—like a movie star. She moved gracefully. Max had said once that watching her was like watching poetry in action—then he'd turned red and denied saying anything and had pounded Joey into the dirt when he'd first tried teasing Max about it.

However, unlike Joey's sister, Linda didn't seem to notice just how beautiful she was. She had Max by the nose, but as far as Joey could see, had never played with him or been cruel to him.

Everyone would have forgiven her if she had been mean—she was so beautiful. But somehow her parents had raised her right.

That didn't mean that Joey wasn't automatically nervous when she came up to him.

"What's up?" Joey asked.

"That's what I wanted to ask you, actually," Linda said.

"What do you mean?" Joey asked, worried. She wasn't going to ask him, like Ma or Da did, about the magic, was she?

Linda sighed, looked down at her hands, one clenched tightly over the other. "What's up with Max?" she asked softly. "He barely talks with me anymore. Won't look at me. Not like he did. Won't…you know."

"I didn't know," Joey said. "Any of that. I haven't seen him around much either. I thought he was hanging out with you."

At that, Linda looked up, her usually soft brown eyes looking hard. "See, I thought the same. That he was hanging out with you. But today, he's over there." She waved toward the edge of the field, closest to the trees. "Kind of off on his own, really."

Joey caught sight of Max immediately. "Huh," he said. It was all he could think to say. What was Max doing all the way over there? Though the field had been blessed by The Fanged One, it still wasn't safe near the woods, particularly not where there were trees draped with thin sheets of white *myst*.

The *myst* couldn't cross the barrier put up by The Fanged One. However, it still wasn't safe.

"I'll go talk with him," Joey told Linda.

"Thank you," Linda said.

Joey slid past an immovable set of adults in deep discussion about field rotation, then had to pause while two kids, chasing each other, ran past. The spring sunshine had stuck around for much of the afternoon, but the clouds gathered on the horizon earlier were starting to spill across the sky.

Max stood with his back to the woods, looking back across the field at all the families celebrating. He drank steadily from a cup—probably either the hard cider or the mead. His face was flushed and he kept looking over his shoulder as if he expected the *myst* to suddenly appear right next to him.

Something was wrong with Max.

"Hey," Joey said, raising his glass to Max, then standing beside him, looking back.

"Hey," Max said. They stood in silence for a while, before Max finally spoke up. "Do you ever wonder why they continue?" he asked.

"Not sure what you mean, buddy," Joey replied.

"I mean, the world *collapsed*. Fell down in pieces around them. All their modern advances demolished with a push of a button somewhere. Some dirty bombs that blew open the rifts, let the *myst* in. Yet, here they are." Max raised his cup as if to toast them. "Celebrating the start of another year."

"Lot of people did die," Joey pointed out. "Die every year. No one actually remembers how it was before." His great-great-great-great grandfather (or was it five greats?) had lived in that old world. Not Joey, or anyone he knew.

"But we do remember!" Max exclaimed.

Joey looked at Max sideways. Was he drunk?

"It's easy enough to touch the past," Max said. He pointed to one of the dividing walls in the field, made of chunks of old concrete. "We're buried in it. There's too much of it. We can't let go enough to live in the present. We always have one foot in the past."

Joey shrugged. It was an old complaint. The adults were too worried about the *myst* to even go out at night. They spoke of Seattle as if it had been a magical place. They'd never been there. Seattle had been swallowed by the Great Inland Sea.

"We have to destroy it," Max said darkly.

"Wait, what?" Joey asked, surprised. "What do you mean, destroy?"

Max finally turned to face Joey. His eyes glowed golden and mad. "Burn them all," he said.

"No," Joey whispered. Not Max. Not his best friend.

Max couldn't go *wyrd* on him.

When had it happened? How had it happened? It shouldn't have been able to happen, not inside the protected barrier put up by The Fanged One that morning.

"We have to destroy them all," Max told Joey. "Come. Help me." He held out his hand to Joey. His fingertips were lit with red and gold flames, glowing lightly in the sunlight.

"No," Joey said, stepping back. "I won't help you."

"Then you will be the first to die," Max said gleefully. He lunged at Joey. Wrapped his hands around Joey's neck.

Joey's skin burned where Max touched him. "Help!" he shouted as loudly as he could. He pulled at Max's hands.

But the *pain*. Sinking into his chest. Running from his palms up his arms. It was like his skin was melting off his bones. Burning.

"HELP!"

Joey kicked Max. His boot struck Max's shin firmly.

More pain.

It was like kicking a rock wall.

Joey kept fighting. Tearing at Max's hands. His arms. Trying to push Max away. Grabbing for his face. His crazed eyes.

Harder to breathe now. Max was choking him. He *had* to get away.

Burning. Burning. He was going to burn and never see the blue-dragon-egg rocks hatch.

*Fight fire with fire.*

Joey would never be able to say where that idea came from.

But he erupted in flames.

Blue flames.

Max staggered back. The blue flames had already leaped from Joey to Max, burning him.

Melting him.

A sane person would have tried to beat at the flames. Tried to put them out.

Max merely laughed.

Joey's own flames died down as quickly as they'd started. He'd find out later that they'd healed all his wounds, including his broken toe.

Max burned and kept burning. Laughing maniacally all the while.

Joey's family and the rest of the town gathered behind him. They stood in shocked silence as Max burned, melting before their eyes.

The smell was sour, like garbage burning. White, not black, smoke rose from Max, as if he'd been filled with *myst* that was now being released

When Max crumbled to the ground, the flames didn't spread. The grass and the ground didn't burn.

Just him.

Joey finally turned to his da, standing beside him. "I didn't mean…I had to…"

"We know, son," Da said, reaching up to squeeze Joey's shoulder.

Joey automatically took a step back. Memories of pain still echoed across his skin.

"Sorry," Da said, glancing at Joey's face then averting his eyes.

Were Joey's eyes glowing golden? Was he already a magician? He didn't feel like a magician. He felt *bad* that he'd had to hurt Max, his best friend since forever.

Linda came up. She at least looked Joey directly in the eye. "He'd gone *wyrd*, hadn't he?" she asked bluntly.

Joey nodded.

Linda started crying and turned back to her family.

"Let's go home," Da told Joey.

What had once been Max was now a pile of white ash. Winds out of nowhere swirled them up and carried them out of the field.

"Why did he go *wyrd*?" Joey asked, looking back over his shoulder as he and his family walked back across the field.

"No one knows why some people go *wyrd*," Ma replied. "Just some people can't handle the magic they call."

Max hadn't called magic, had he? "Why would Max try to call magic? Why would he want to be a magician?" Joey asked.

"He was trying to be like you. Idiot," his sister said.

Joey flinched at her tone, though that made even less sense to him. But he held his tongue.

By the time they returned to their house, and Joey checked in the mirror, his eyes had gone back to normal.

How long before they'd turn golden permanently?

## *Fourteen*

arl didn't want to go view The Mountain and His changes.

He didn't have a choice.

Jim went meekly along with the group, walking up to the viewing platform, standing with *Carl's* brothers (not Jim's!) and observing The Mountain.

Carl knew it was a sham. Jim was not meek. He always did everything for a reason. Generally, not a good reason.

It wasn't raining. The summer had been dry. The Mountain stood before Carl in all His glory. A few sparse clouds wreathed His top, like a fluffy crown. The base stood solid and tinged with blue. Trees closer to New Mountain Town had a touch of *myst* that morning.

Carl longed to leave. He fidgeted, which brought him disapproving stares from the brothers standing on either side of him.

Jim made him stay. Made him keep his gaze on The Mountain.

Made him not look away when the *myst* came, obscuring their view, stealing the Voice of The Mountain again.

Carl shuddered as the alien feelings poured in. The hatred. The greed. The need to destroy.

Jim felt some of those things already. But not as much. Not as intensely.

All of Carl's brothers stirred, as if they took a large breath together.

The *myst* suddenly manifested in New Mountain Town, on the platform. It settled in around them, wrapping them in cool dampness.

With so many captured at the same time, the *myst* formed words, not just emotions.

Carl froze in terror when the *myst* said his name.

"Yes?" he asked. He couldn't help but reply, though all he wanted to do was run away.

*I need a general.*

"I'm not smart enough," Carl said. He'd always been slow.

*We'll make you smart enough.*

Thoughts, concepts, ideas, plans, unfolded in Carl's head. He could suddenly see how to make the camp better, more efficient. How to schedule all the men around their viewing time. The best way to plant the crops to use the land to its fullest.

And beyond. He suddenly *knew* things. Like how to make the hard stone that the ancient people made. How to build those long bridges.

How to fly.

Carl longed for these things. Longed to be smart, deep in his bones, all the way to his toes. Longed to help not just New Mountain Town but the entire world with all this knowledge. Things he could apply to every town and village he visited. People would no longer shun him. He'd have brothers who would follow him. Women, too, if he wanted.

But Jim wanted things too. How to make the guns work. How to forge steel. How to make flame that never died.

Carl fought to forget. To let go of those things. To not remember the easiest ways to kill a man, how to drown someone in their own blood, how to rip out a tongue, the feel of gore on his sword.

Jim fought back.

Jim won.

Jim/Carl stepped off the platform. He felt ravenous. His hands were already formed into claws, and his teeth gnashed together.

"My brothers!" he called out. His voice was so clear now!

As were his thoughts. His *plans.*

"We will cleanse the world of the scum of Man! Bring the call of night! Let the earth and The Mountain have their rightful place in a pure world!"

His brothers agreed, hooting and howling, calling for death and blood, their golden eyes gleaming.

Little Carl, drowning far inside the hate and greed, felt as doomed as the rest of the world.

# Fifteen

Saul poked his head into Manuel's office. "Boss? You gotta come see this."

Manuel sighed and put down the chalk, glancing at the four boards now filled with schedules and scribbles. Everything was getting so complicated. It was getting impossible to keep track of every man and woman, making sure that the work was split fairly, along with the viewing time. The newcomers still needed more time with the mountain.

"What is it?" Manuel asked.

But Saul hadn't stuck around. He'd gone back outside already.

That wasn't like Saul at all. Perplexed, Manuel rose, grabbed his hat, and went outside.

What in blazes was Saul on about? Manuel didn't see anything special. Men were coming and going, as normal. Fred was carrying a large sack of flour toward the kitchen area for the bread. The sky was mostly clear, the summer day cooler—sure signs that fall was on its way.

But then Manuel watched as Ben walked into Fred's path, reached out and touched him, laying both hands on Fred's shoulders.

Why would Ben touch Fred like that? People didn't even shake hands.

Fred shook as if jolted, just once. Then he put down the sack and followed Ben, going toward the viewing platform.

What the hell? That wasn't normal at all.

Manuel followed them, fear sinking deep into the pit of his stomach.

A deep rumbling came from the men gathered before the viewing platform, with more coming in. Manuel recognized one of the teams that should be tending the fields.

They stood there, growling, occasionally howling.

The anger that poured off them made Manuel stagger back.

They weren't viewing the mountain. They milled around, walking up to each other, each grasping the shoulder of the other, then moving on.

It wasn't until Manuel got a little closer that he realized they all had golden eyes.

They'd gone *wyrd*. Every one of them. They were all mad and crazy and *dangerous* as all get out.

Had the mountain made them that way? Or had it just made them vulnerable?

A cloud of *myst* formed over them, tendrils dropping down to touch one, then another, on the head.

Manuel started backing away.

Too late.

They'd noticed him. Had turned toward him.

Manuel started to run.

## *Sixteen*

Lady Liberty swung her torch at the encroaching *myst*, forcing it back. The summer had been dry in her area that year, though to the south, closer to The Mountain, there had been more rain. If she used her flames, there was a chance the nearby trees could catch fire. She danced over to the next tree, her green toes just touching the slim branches, then pushed the *myst* back more.

The *myst* had been more aggressive all summer, encroaching everywhere it could. Lady Liberty had fought hard to keep the woods clear of the *myst* and safe for her people, as well as all the travelers who came along her portion of the west coast trade route.

It was funny—though she'd been a statue in the ancient times, before the bombs had opened the rifts, letting the *myst* pour through—she still remembered those days. Remembered standing on the side of the Interstate, the cars pouring past her as they drove from Seattle to Portland and back. She'd had no thoughts at that time. Certainly couldn't have spoken or moved.

But she'd watched the highways. Watched over travelers. And when the world changed, she'd changed as well.

She'd been created as a man-sized statue. Now, she was easily twice that height. When she'd first woken, it was because the *myst* had drawn around her. Suddenly, her torch had flamed brightly, burning it away.

But in order to fight, she'd put down the tablet she'd once carried in the center of the old highway. It had instantly grown to be as wide as the road, and three hundred yards long, becoming what men now called Tablet Road.

The *myst* couldn't abide Tablet Road. It couldn't even drift over it. It always had to pass around it, either to the north or the south.

As the years passed and the road retreated under the onslaught of green until it became a mere trail, Tablet Road stayed clear. Trees grew up around it, their roots digging into the concrete on either side, but nothing grew on the road itself.

Men used the old highways for the trade route. There weren't many at first, just ones and twos. At first, they'd avoided Tablet Road, unsure of its properties.

As the woods grew and proper traders started up and down the coast, they'd marveled at the clear space. They'd also noticed the *myst's* aversion to it. They'd spent a night on the road, safe.

They'd also left the next day, shaken by their dreams.

Lady Liberty wasn't certain what they'd dreamed of. Had it been the past? Did ancient echoes of the cars and semis make them restless? Or had they dreamed of the date that her tablet had once carried, a date now once celebrated with fireworks and picnics, now as obsolete as the ancient vehicles?

Tablet Road was the only place in Lady Liberty's territory where she could rest, now. There had been other, more clear areas, once. They'd been overrun by the *myst* long ago.

Even when she rested there, the *myst* still harried her at night, crouching along the edges, hissing.

Lady Liberty chased the most recent attack of the *myst* across the treetops, skipping easily after it, her green robes flowing in the wind.

The *myst* withdrew, drawing her toward the north, then spread out again, coating the tops of *her* trees.

Lady Liberty took a step toward it, then hesitated.

Something wasn't right.

She turned. She'd been fighting the *myst* most of the morning. She hadn't realized just how far it had drawn her. She was at the northernmost area of her territory, on the border of The Painted One. Not that he would have minded Lady Liberty coming into his area. But they had an agreement of sorts not to fight too much on each other's lands.

The *myst* had been drawing her out that way, deliberately. Lady Liberty saw the pattern now. It had lost parts of itself, yes, but mainly it had been leading her away.

Away from what?

Something was happening on the southern part of her territory.

Something bad.

Lady Liberty did something she'd never done before.

She turned her back to the *myst* and fled.

The growling and howling was clear, even through the trees. What would make such a noise? Why hadn't she heard it before? Had the *myst* she'd been fighting clouded her mind?

Lady Liberty was stunned when she dropped beneath the trees. There was a group of men—the largest group she'd seen traveling, more than a thousand, stretching out along the trade route.

They weren't themselves though. They were little better than moving parts of the *myst*.

And maybe that was the point.

The first wave of men had reached the southern edge of Tablet Road. They'd brought picks with them, old steel tools made solid and new through magic, and were smashing the edges of the tablet.

They were trying to destroy it. *Myst* floated above them, tendrils reaching down to touch the heads of one or another as they continued their destruction.

Lady Liberty dropped down, appearing before them. *Stop,* she commanded.

She didn't speak—she'd never been able to speak. But she could communicate well enough.

They laughed at her.

They weren't really men. She flew at them, brandishing her torch, the flames burning brightly, burning the *myst* that floated above them.

They attacked her with their pikes and sledgehammers and mattocks.

Lady Liberty stumbled back, stunned. She'd never been attacked by *men* before. Worshipped and feared, yes.

But these weren't men. They were controlled by the *myst*. As evil as her old adversary.

Lady Liberty flew up higher for a moment. More and more of these *myst* men, this horde, stumbled through the trees.

She would lose. There were too many of them.

Still, she flew back down to the head of the column and flamed the men she could, fighting on, trying to stop them as she had tried to stop the *myst* all these years, despite the battle being hopeless.

What would happen when she fell? Not to her—when she was gone, she'd be gone—but to The Painted One, and all the towns they protected between them?

## Seventeen

Abraham squatted down next to the roots of the great pine. A circle of *csípős* mushrooms! These looked good, too. The caps were bright red, with little white dots. He broke off the edge of one with his fingernails. Huh. He hadn't realized they'd grown so long and claw-like. Maybe he'd have to do something about that the next time he went into town.

The mushroom smelled earthy, without a hint of its sharp taste.

Had they transformed as well? It had been last spring since he'd been mushroom hunting.

He cautiously put the edge of the mushroom on his tongue.

Instantly, his mouth was on fire. There was no other taste.

These would do nicely in stew.

Abraham was aware that Kris and Sa'id, the other magicians in his area, rarely ate anymore. They lived on magic and *myst*, like the small gods that protected every human settlement up and down the coast. They weren't stronger magicians than he was, necessarily. But they were far less human.

Abraham liked to eat. He didn't cook often, but he was in the mood for stew. Fall had recently started, the nights turning refreshingly cool.

Abraham flooded his mouth with water from the inside, calling on his own body to wash away the sharp burn from the mushroom. Only then could he taste it, a warm bitterness. He'd have to get some carrots, maybe trade for some beets, in order to balance it.

The mushrooms carefully went into the bag Abraham wore, cushioned next to the wild coltsfoot he'd found that would go into a charm for pregnant women, to help them keep their babies.

A crash farther in the woods made Abraham look up from his hunt. Was it Crested Cook, coming back along the path? Abraham hoped it was—he'd like to thank him for widening the path and making it safer for Abraham, letting him more easily access a deeper part of the woods.

He stood up, his hands cupped, the magic in his soul warming quickly. He had heard about a pack of bears come down from the mountain earlier—not rabid and *myst*-controlled, but far too canny. He didn't plan on becoming part of a bear's stew.

Then a howl split the quiet of the woods.

A human howl.

Abraham set his bag down at the roots of the pine tree. He set his hand against the bark, leaving a magical marker there so he could find it again later. The magic would also alert the *myst* that something special was there, but he'd fight it if he had to. The *csípős* mushrooms were too rare to accidentally crush.

Then Abraham took off, calling on his magic to aid his feet, making his way along the path quickly, going toward the loud howl. He didn't feel fear—he couldn't remember the last time he felt fear. Maybe an edge of excitement, though. Plus curiosity, the one emotion that seemed to remain true despite how much magic he used.

A growling noise rumbled through the air.

What was making that noise? Abraham's curiosity grew.

He followed the growls and howls when it veered off the trail, into the denser woods, slowing as the underbrush grew thick. Everything under the trees grew so fast, encouraged by the *myst*, to make the woods seem impenetrable.

Abraham had always wondered if that was a conscious plan of the *myst*, to keep man hemmed in to small areas.

A clearing opened up under the trees. Abraham stopped just at the edge, not stepping out into the open.

Crested Cook fought a group of men. His feathered rainbow crest was fully extended, the blades in the colorful feathers flashing. The crest ran from the small god's forehead, across the top of his bald head, then all the way down his spine to form a tail that swept the ground.

But parts of the crest were already thinned. Crested Cook plucked a knife-feather from his crest and threw it at one of the men.

The man gasped and fell back.

Abraham watched the man's eyes go from bright golden to muddy brown.

All the other men still had golden eyes.

Another man came up and touched the injured man's shoulder.

His eyes turned golden again, and he rejoined the fight.

It was an entire army of men, with a few women, who had gone *wyrd*.

Farther back along the line of men still pouring into the clearing, Abraham saw a cloud of *myst* above them. A thin thread of white dropped down and touched the tallest man. He had curly gray hair and a jaw that wasn't hinged right.

Who was that? Though his eyes proclaimed him as *wyrd* as the others, he still seemed to maintain more consciousness. He swept his arm out, directing the other men.

He was planning on surround Crested Cook. Overwhelming the small god with crazed men.

A chill took over Abraham. A man who could talk with the *myst*? Act as a general for this horde?

Abraham hadn't known fear in a long, long time.

He knew fear now.

Could Abraham destroy him? This general was defended by the *myst*, but not much else. And the rest of the men hadn't seen Abraham yet.

Abraham gathered the magic inside of him, careful not to draw anything from outside of himself. He couldn't tap any other sources. It might alert the horde.

He'd learned long ago how to burn away the *myst*. He couldn't destroy large swaths of it, like a small god. He could sometimes clear away a small patch, however. Keep his small hut safe.

Abraham remembered the burning sensation of the *csípős* mushrooms. Remembered how it had felt as though he'd put a burning ember on his tongue. Gathered all that fire into himself, building it, fanning it hotter. Building a condensed ball of unstoppable flames.

Then he flung it across the clearing.

Surprisingly, the ball hit his target. The tall man was momentarily covered in red-hot flames. The men beside him fell back, screaming.

Their flames had to be put out by their companions.

That was interesting. The *wyrd* generally wanted to die.

The general—he *absorbed* the flames. His burned skin healed immediately.

He turned his clear golden eyes directly toward Abraham. He didn't say anything. Just pointed.

More fear. Abraham turned and started running.

When Abraham made it back to his shack, he didn't stop to congratulate himself. It was only a matter of time before the *myst* horde swept out of the woods like a tidal wave, destroying everything in its path.

He had to warn people of what was coming. What was rolling up the coast toward them, along the trade-route roads.

Abraham quickly collected a few things—extra shoes for his journey. A cloak for the rain. As many dried, powdered herbs he could easily carry, anything that would help his magic. An ancient spyglass, well preserved with magic, that he could use to see things in the distance.

He was going to need all the help he could get.

The only time he paused was when he started putting a sketch pad into his bag.

It wasn't necessary. He was going to be tired enough, constantly on the move, probably until he made a mistake and the *myst* army killed him. It was one more thing to carry, one more thing to protect, to keep dry and clean.

He took it anyway. He might no longer be human, but it was his connection to humanity. He couldn't let it go. Maybe it was why he still ate as he did.

Then Abraham took off, racing up the trade route, heading to the closet town.

He didn't know if his warnings would be heeded. If they would do any good. What the men in the towns could do to fight an army controlled by the *myst*.

They deserved the chance to try.

# Eighteen

Ima waited in the middle of the old road, where cars used to go. Trees bunched near the edges, and a few had found a way to break through the concrete. Sunlight tried valiantly to burn through the fall haze covering the sky. Ima was glad it couldn't reach her.

The small god in the area had kept the road clear. No wonder it had had to die.

Birds hidden in the trees chittered and scolded her for being so exposed. She wasn't about to hide. Since that fateful night when her father had locked her in the barn, she hadn't hid once. Certainly not from him, showing him her claws and teeth and strength as she took his life from him.

She hadn't bothered to hide from the town Elders either. Not exactly. She'd waited for two days—they'd come quicker than she'd thought—then strode out into the yard while they were inside. The *myst* directed the spark she pulled up, into an old line that hadn't been shut down properly. That still held remnants of smelly gas.

The *myst* hadn't been certain that Ima could set fire to the gas.

Ima had proved that she was The One, that the *myst* had saved the right girl, letting her keep her soul and her thoughts, not turning her completely *wyrd* and wild.

The explosion she'd caused had knocked her on her ass.

But the Elders had deserved it. They hadn't saved her from her father. She'd had to save herself. They should have known what type of man he'd become.

If she could, she'd do it all over again. And again. And again.

The *myst* helped get her through the woods, turning away the wildcats who tracked her, then directing her to another cabin. The magician there was easy enough to slaughter. She wasn't really human, anyway.

Or at least that was what Ima told herself as she proved herself again to the *myst*, showed it that she could be its champion.

In return, Ima never had to be afraid of anything. She'd found creatures in the woods that she'd only ever heard stories about, wolf monsters with eight legs who belched nasty-smelling smoke, or human-sized birds who tried to wave her away with their wings.

She'd killed them too.

But instead of directing her to another house or farther into the woods, this time, the *myst* had her wait on the road.

Off in the distance, Ima heard a rumbling noise. It grew louder, into a howling, growling sound. It made Ima's heart pound faster. What the hell was that?

But she wasn't about to hide. She just knew she was supposed to wait. The *myst* had been very clear about that. Just wait. And so she did, showing the *myst* that she could listen as well as direct her own path.

She didn't have to wait for long. Five men came running down the old road, skimming around the few trees that had popped up. All of them had the hated golden eyes of magicians, but they also had claws and fangs, like her. They wore torn and stained clothes, as if they'd been living in the woods for a while. Their shoes and boots were still solid and firm, however.

The first man ran right up to Ima, stopping mere inches away. He didn't reach out to touch her, but just stared.

God, he smelled rank. Ima stood her ground. She even put her arms over her chest. *Oh yeah?*

The man stepped back. He grunted at her.

Ima nodded in reply.

She knew that while he'd understand words, he wouldn't be able to use them. She'd been losing her own ability—something the *myst* had taken. She hadn't really missed them much.

One of the five turned and raced back along the road. Soon, more men spilled out of the woods, in ones and twos and fives and tens. A few women as well. They stayed piled up, several yards away.

An ugly man came up the road finally. He was really tall, with curly gray hair and a face that wasn't right, something about his jaw. A weird light lit his eyes, beyond the gold, making them seem more than human.

He nodded at her, his head bobbing. "Carl," he said, his voice rough.

"Ima," she replied.

Carl held out his hand to Ima. It was clean—much cleaner than her own. It wasn't as much of a claw as hers, either.

She still hesitated. Somewhere inside her was a little girl still screaming for her daddy, not the grotesque creature he'd become with his skin hanging in strips, but the one who tucked her in at night, kissed her on the forehead, and told her he'd protect her from all the monsters.

But that was in her past. She couldn't live there. She could only go forward.

Ima took Carl's hand. Images rocketed through her. Towns that had been destroyed. Battles waged and won. How after they cleared the coast, they'd turn inland, sweep across the country.

Clear the world of all those who opposed them.

Carl dropped Ima's hand and she fell into line behind him. Part of her was gleeful with all the killing ahead. She'd happily join the men for that. Direct her sparks where they needed to go. Make the whole world burn.

But a part of her was bitter as well. The *myst* had chosen *her*. She was the important one. She was to be the champion. The one whose hands the *myst* needed and used.

She was supposed to be The One.

Not Carl. Not him.

She knew the *myst* wasn't stupid like the Elders, thinking that only men could do the important tasks. But she still didn't understand why the *myst* thought it needed Carl.

She'd just have to bide her time. Watch for her opportunity. Take over when Carl failed, either by his own mistake or by her doing.

Prove that she was The One.

# Nineteen

The horde is coming."

Joey shivered at Abraham's announcement. He stood in the market square with Ma and Da and his brothers and sisters. Fall had come fast that year: It seemed as though most of the trees had changed colors in a single week, then the rain had brought down all the leaves.

The fall witch still delighted in the colored leaves—Joey hadn't been able to sleep and had gone to the window to watch her dance across the field where the leaves had fallen.

But there wouldn't be many that year. She wouldn't be very strong. There wouldn't be long tunnels through the woods protected from the *myst*, just short ones.

"They're destroying everything in their path. Turning the people they can. They've doubled in number since I first saw them," Abraham told them, his golden eyes glowing against his dark skin. He had a long, goat-like face, with the buds of horns sticking out of his temples.

"The Fanged One—" interrupted Tom, who Ma and Da referred to as the mayor of Lakeland.

"Will be slaughtered as well," Abraham said solemnly. "I watched them destroy Crested Cook, our own small god."

Stunned silence followed.

"There are too many of them," Abraham said.

"Why didn't you help?" Tom asked.

Abraham sighed. "I tried. Tried to destroy the leader. Tall man. Curly hair. Face looks wrong. He shrugged off the fire like it was water."

"Maybe if you and Terri—" Tom started.

"I need to keep heading north. To warn the other towns," Abraham said firmly. "The horde has kept to a single course, up the trade route along the coast. The other towns deserve a chance to fight or flee as well."

Joey looked at the others standing there. What should they do? Try to defend Lakeville? Or should they run?

Running wouldn't be much safer, not with the way the *myst* had been expanding.

But an army…

"What about the Great Inland Sea?" Joey asked. He couldn't help himself. He'd always been curious about what had happened to Billy the Bard, if he'd asked his questions, or if the sea had just swallowed him whole.

Abraham turned his inhuman eyes toward Joey. "The what?"

Joey felt exposed as the people around him shifted away, clearing a path between him and the magician. "The Sound overran her banks and swallowed the city of Seattle," he said. "She absorbed all the knowledge of the city and turned into an oracle. She calls herself the Great Inland Sea."

Abraham nodded slowly. "I've seen that. The Sound pushing up. Battering the buildings. Wave upon wave."

How had he seen it? There weren't any photographs or movies of it. That was after the rifts. After the *myst*. After the fall of the ancients.

"Should Joey go with you to consult the oracle?" Tom asked Abraham, but he also took a step forward, turning to face the rest of the crowd, asking for their opinion. "While the rest of us prepare to defend the town?"

Joey's apprehension grew, his stomach knotting.

They would fight.

Would they win?

"Joey can go his own," Abraham said quickly. "I travel light. And fast. I can't travel with anyone."

"But Joey here's going to be a magician," Tom said eagerly. "It would be good training for him to go with you. If both of you went to ask the oracle how to stop the horde."

If Joey really had been a magician, he would have disappeared into a hole in the ground right there and then. Everyone was staring at him. He didn't want to become a magician. He'd never wanted it.

"You do have some magic," Abraham pronounced.

"So does everyone else," Joey pointed out quickly. He still didn't want to have to use it. He didn't want to lose his family and his friends, though Max was already gone.

"Come. Or stay. The choice is up to you," Abraham said. "But make it quickly. I must be off."

Joey turned to Da. "What about defending the town?"

Tom spoke up. "Knowledge is as important as walls and lined traps."

"I don't want to lose you," Joey said urgently to his father. He didn't want to be having this conversation with half the town listening in.

"I will always call you my son," Da said. "No matter what changes you go through."

Ma nodded, and said, "And we'll be proud of you."

"This has been your destiny, ever since you told Grandpa Schuller he wasn't holding a blue-dragon-egg rock," Da added.

Suddenly, Abraham was standing beside them. "Blue-dragon-egg rock?"

At Da's nod, Abraham demanded, "Show me."

The entire town traipsed after them, talking in low mutters about the coming battle, already making plans.

Abraham seemed impatient, but he contained his steps and walked with them. Joey wondered if he could just appear and disappear, like Lisel, the wolf-headed magician he'd met.

The tower, or folly, as some in the town still called it, rose high above everything around it, taller than the trees just past the fields. The base of it rambled and had been formed into half a dozen sprawling walls to support the weight of the stones going up.

Most of the stones were round and gray. A mixture of ash, crushed rock, and burned lime—a primitive cement—had been slathered across the lower layers, to hold the rocks together.

The tower narrowed as it climbed. Ledges had been built at each ladder height all the way up. It wasn't evenly hollow. Some places only a small boy could fit inside. There were no stairs and very little internal structure.

More than one person in town had predicted that a strong wind was going to blow the tower down.

But it stayed standing, not even shifting a little during the strongest storms.

Abraham seemed fascinated by it. He didn't say a word, just walked all the way around the walls sticking out of the base to support it, always looking up. He even got out a long adjustable stick, made of wood and brass, and held it up to his eye to look at the top.

Finally he came back to where the rest of them were standing. "Who built this?"

Da stepped forward. "We did." As the head of the Schuller clan, it was his place. "Our family."

"The stones, all the way up. They're all like this?" Abraham said, indicating one of the rocks at the base of the tower. It looked like all the others, about a foot across, oval and gray.

Da gestured Joey to come forward to answer the question.

Joey looked at the rock Abraham pointed out. He could feel it from a few feet away. It didn't pulse or pull at him. He didn't feel compelled to touch it or be close to the rock. He did know it was strong, though.

"Not all of them are that strong, no," Joey admitted.

Da looked bewildered. He hadn't known that, hadn't realized the stones had different strengths.

No one in the family knew the rocks like Joey. Something he'd never bothered to try to explain to them, not while he'd been trying to fit in.

Abraham nodded though. "Why have you collected them all together? What's it for?"

Even Joey hesitated. Through an unspoken agreement, the town had never talked about the blue dragons, never mentioned it to traders or other folks passing through.

Everyone in the town knew—it was why their farm was called The Blue Dragon Farm. But it was still something of a private matter.

Da cleared his throat and spoke up. "Some year, the winter witch will bless the rocks and hatch the blue dragons."

The people closest to Da shifted uneasily. Joey looked at his feet.

"The winter witch?" Abraham asked. "Is she another small god?"

"No, no," Da said quickly. "The witches are different." He explained about how they changed every season, transforming into something new.

Joey listened, surprised. He'd thought he'd been the only one called to the window to watch the witches dance.

Abraham blinked. "I've never seen anything like this. Never heard of it." He turned to Joey. "Stay. Or go. It's your call." He paused, then added. "If you came with me, I'd like to learn more about the witches and the rocks."

Joey swallowed hard. Though magic had filled the edges of his world, he'd known that someday he'd have to make a choice. Magic couldn't just take him. There would have to be a final decision, steps he took on his own.

The town needed information if they were to survive. And Joey was the only one who could get that for them.

"I'll go with you," Joey said quietly.

Ma smiled brilliant through her tears, and Da pulled him into a rough embrace.

Joey didn't have time to say all the things he wanted to, however.

In an hour, he and Abraham were gone.

# Twenty

Erin woke up in deep woods. Tall trees rose above her, thick and overgrown. She smelled dried mulch and pine. When she sat up, she didn't see an obvious trail—just a deer run that she was already dreading following. The sun was declining toward the west and the air was turning still and dusky.

She hated waking up in the woods this way. It generally meant a long trek to somewhere, the *myst* harrying her the entire way. Her clothes and sandals gave her protection from the worst of the creatures and the vines in the woods that would attack her. They couldn't really protect her when the birds decided to drop things on her head.

Fortunately, Erin didn't hear any birds in the nearby trees. She knew she didn't have a lot of time, though. Night would be upon her shortly, and she wanted to be wherever it was she was going before it got fully dark.

She'd never understood why the power that moved her from place to place couldn't just put her next to wherever it was that it wanted her to go. It would have been so much easier that way.

Or, at the very least, tell her *why* she kept being moved. What was she searching for? She'd given herself her mission of talking with magicians.

Erin pushed herself to stand and choose a direction at random. She couldn't actually see the sun, didn't have a clue which way she should go. She hadn't gone far, however, before she smelled a fire.

A cooking fire.

Was there a road nearby? And traders? They were sure to have a magician with them. She'd never been dropped near traders before.

Would they welcome her? She couldn't lie and say she'd come from a nearby town. They'd know something was strange with her. Different.

And being too different got you killed.

Erin approached the camp slowly, trying not to make any noise. She wanted to study them for a while before letting them know she was there.

However, it didn't appear to be a big group. Traders generally had a dozen people with them, as well as carts of goods and either oxen or horses to pull them.

There was only a single person though—a cute guy—sitting alone, next to the fire. He was feeding it dried twigs in between turning a skewered rabbit on a makeshift spit.

He had normal human eyes. Kind. Pale blue. His face was tanned from working outside and his hands looked big and rough—probably a farm kid. She'd bet he hadn't been on the road for long. His clothes looked too clean, almost new, in fact.

What was he doing here in the middle of the woods? Had some power dropped him there as well?

Erin sighed. She'd never find out hiding in the woods.

It was still hard to make herself step forward. She kept her hand wrapped around the haft of her knife, tucked into the rope belt tied around her shapeless brown robe.

Erin had almost reached the fire before the young man looked up. He leaped to his feet, startled.

Blue fire danced across the tips of his fingertips.

So he *was* a magician. But still learning. Not fully transformed.

Had his town forced him to leave? Was he still setting up his shack or hut?

"Hello," Erin said. She held her head up and stared directly at him to show she wasn't afraid, though her heart pounded hard in her chest.

"Hello," the young man said cautiously. "Where the blazes did you come from?"

For a brief moment, Erin was tempted to tell him the truth. What would it matter? She'd be gone in the morning.

But she wanted to ask him questions, not have him just ask her about things she didn't know, had never been able to even guess.

"I got lost," she lied. "I was trying to make it Hwa Hung's trailer—you know, the magician? But there was this cloud of *myst* and I ran into the woods and I've been lost all afternoon."

It was almost the truth. She *had* been on her way to the trailer of her town's local magician. Her mother had sent her to ask for blessings on the sachets her mother had made.

Then a cloud of *myst* had boiled across the road.

Before Erin could turn and run, something had swooped her up. A hand, maybe. Or a wing. She was never quite sure, had never been able to remember precisely.

She'd awoken in the woods, strangely dressed, and with nothing to do but try to find her way home. She knew she'd grown up somewhere with mountains to the west.

She missed the mountains.

The young man, however, believed her story. He snuffed out the flames on his fingertips and gestured for her to come closer. "Please, would you like something to eat? There's more here than I can manage," he said.

She suspected he was lying—if he was anything like her brothers had been, he was probably always hungry.

But so was she. "Thank you," she said, stepping forward into the light.

"I'm Joey," the young man said. He put his palms together over his chest and bowed his head to her.

Erin copied the gesture. It hadn't been how she'd been raised to greet another person, but she was adaptable. She'd seen it before. This gesture was generally used near the west coast. "I'm Erin."

"Would you like to join me for dinner?" Joey asked, gallantly offering her a seat next to the fire.

"Thank you," Erin said. She hoped her strange hair wouldn't prompt too many questions. She didn't really have an excuse for why one side was short and the other long—she'd done it herself in rebellion against the force dropping her here and there.

It had been a while since she'd eaten. Magicians didn't always eat, or remember to invite her to dine with them when they did.

"So what's the closest town?" Joey asked. "We're here to warn them."

"Warn them? About what?" Erin asked, curious. What could be worse than what any town was sure to already be dealing with?

Joey explained about the horde making its way up the coast.

"How did you survive the attack of the horde?" Erin asked. If they were that powerful, Joey must have had some strong defenses. Or maybe they'd bypassed his town?

"He didn't," came a voice out of the darkness. Another man strode forward.

Erin silently cursed. She should have realized that Joey wasn't strong enough to survive the woods on his own. And hadn't he just said "we"? She should have been paying more attention.

The man stepped closer, into the light.

"I know you," he said, his golden eyes flashing.

# Twenty-One

Spira sagged against the trees already bare of their wonderful leaves. *Come back!* she wanted to shout. *Don't leave me!*

But Joey still hugged his parents, brothers, and sister. Then he walked away, up the trader's trail, away from the farm and toward the north.

Spira could follow Joey all the way to Seattle. It would weaken her much more than she already was, though. Too many trees hadn't changed the color of their leaves—they'd just browned and fallen. And Spira needed the colors to fuel her change, to fuel her fight against the *myst*, to keep her alive through the season.

At least her sister, the summer witch, had left Spira with enough energy to start the season. The summer witches were the luckiest, as far as Spira was concerned: All that sunshine and nothing to spend it on. While Spira had to tuck away as much energy as she could so her next sister could survive the coming winter.

Why had Joey left? Was it something to do with the coming horde of *wyrd* men, destroying everything in their path? It was supposed to be the *myst* that finished the destruction of man. Not his fellow man.

They weren't ready yet! None of the witches were, or the small gods. They were all doomed.

Spira stayed at the tops of the trees, though a part of her wanted to dip down, let the vines along the forest floor catch her and tear her to pieces. It might hurt less than the final battle.

Despondent, Spira sang to herself, making the tree limbs sway. *Da dee, da dah, da dum.* None of the other men in the family were as sensitive as Joey. He was the only one she could talk to, that her sisters had sung to. He was the only one who listened to their news, even if he rarely came to the window to watch them dance.

Why couldn't he just stay here? Why had he turned away from her?

Not that Spira could do that much. She could loan the rocks some of her energy, what little she had. They were growing, growing into something that would help man. But she wasn't supposed to hatch them. That was up to her sister.

Was it finally time? Was that why Joey had left? Or had he just abandoned them?

As night fell, Spira drifted up from the trees, toward the dark sky. She rose and rose, the air turning colder every foot she rose. Thinner, too. Would it support her if she kept going? Or would she fall?

Did it matter? Joey was gone.

Spira hummed a sad tune and spiraled back down to the few leaves she could find, sucking up their energy. How long would she last? How long would her sisters?

She went from her leaves to the tower, the rocks calling out her. They promised safety. They promised shelter.

They lied.

They would protect her from the *myst,* but at such a cost.

Spira still settled down, spreading her dandelion skirts wide over the rocks. They weren't as strong up here, except for the few that Joey had chosen. The family had been failing until him.

She resisted settling anything but her weight on the rocks, hoarding her energy and magic. She wouldn't give the tower any of the *spark* that it wanted.

The humans would just have to wait until her sister came to help the rocks grow.

Or until Joey came back.

Hopefully he'd come back in time.

# Twenty-Two

Abraham stirred the fire's embers with magic, ready to fling flames and burning coals at this Erin. He'd judged her human. She still looked it.

She must have fooled him, though. Must have somehow deceived his eyes. How was she doing that? How could she use such strong magic without appearing to?

She wore the same brown homespun robe, tied with a crude belt around her waist. A knife stuck out of the side, her hand wrapped tightly around the hilt. Her hair was still crudely cut, one side hacked up above her ear while the other hung down past her shoulder.

As far as he could see, she was absolutely not magical. But there was no possible way for anyone not magical to appear out here in the middle of the wilderness without magic.

Abraham felt an intense curiosity, warring with his caution.

"It's not what you think," Erin told them both, her eyes wide and wild, darting from him to Joey who was now standing, and back again. Was she scared? If she was that powerful, why was she scared?

"Then explain it," Abraham said. He wasn't going to let her run. He was too curious.

But if he wasn't satisfied with her story, he would feed her to the flames.

"I don't know how I got here," Erin said.

Abraham couldn't contain his growl. That wasn't good enough. He set the flames sparking. Out of the corner of his eye he saw a blue flame spring up in Joey's hands.

"I don't!" she said, her eyes growing more wide. "I was going down the road. Like I told you," she said, nodding at Joey.

Abraham looked at Joey. He nodded.

So Erin had told Joey some other story, closer to the truth than what she'd told with him.

"There was a huge pool of *myst* across it. Then I was someplace else. And the next day. And the next. Every day." She turned to Abraham, pleading. "I wasn't lying when I asked for you to teach me magic. I need to learn. I need to figure out how to get back home."

Abraham looked at her curiously. "You know I would have helped you if you'd told me the truth," he said.

Erin shook her head. "No, you wouldn't have. You would have held me. Tried to see what it was that was moving me. That's what other magicians did. The first two I told."

Abraham shrugged. She may have been right. He was curious.

"Why do you go from place to place, seeking out magicians?" Abraham asked.

"I don't know!" Erin said. "I told you. I just get dropped. I was the one who decided to find magicians."

Was the girl telling the truth? She was very good at lying. Abraham couldn't tell.

Of course, Joey would believe her. Abraham had never known someone so trusting. He certainly didn't remember being like that when he'd been a boy.

Then again, Joey was the most human magician Abraham had ever met. He held onto his normalcy with tight fists, refusing to do even the slightest sliver of magic unless he was forced into it. The flames dancing on his fingertips had been the first that Abraham had seen.

"What did you do with my notebook?" Abraham asked.

Erin shook her head. "I didn't take it. Please, believe me. I wouldn't ever take anything from a magician!"

The girl carried nothing, not food, not a bag, not even a comb. She appeared as she had the first time he'd met her, too thin, too pale, and too scared.

That she appeared to know nothing about his notebook made her story more believable.

"You may join us, then," Abraham said, releasing the fire, letting its brightness die down to a normal level.

Joey shot him a surprised look. "Okay," he said. He brushed his hands down his thighs.

Abraham nodded. When the girl left in the morning, he'd have to ask Joey about the flames he called. All the fire Abraham called was normal-colored, red and gold.

Joey's flames were pure blue.

The three of them sat in stilted silence around the crackling flames while Joey finished roasting the spitted rabbit. "Would you like some?" Joey asked Abraham as he removed it from the fire.

"No," Abraham said. He could eat, he was hungry, but he didn't really need it tonight. Tomorrow, perhaps, he'd refuel his body with food instead of magic. Both Joey and the girl were much more hungry and needed the rabbit more.

He'd been correct. He was surprised at how neat they both were, tearing off legs to get at the meat, then cracking the bones and sucking out the marrow.

While they ate, Abraham went back under the trees. It wasn't quite fully dark—his eyes enabled him to see better than humans—but he still didn't linger. It wasn't safe away from the fire, even for him. But he found a gourd that he split and roasted as he carried it back, handing half each to Joey and Erin.

The two of them grinned and fell to, demolishing the sweet pulp, scrapping it out of the soft shell with fingernails, getting every last bit.

"Thank you," Erin said as she finished, tossing the remains on the fire.

"You're welcome," Abraham said. "Now, tell me about where you grew up. Every detail you remember."

Erin complied, telling him about the town square, the flatlands, the mountains to the west, the ways the winds came from the north, carrying rain and snow. How the Masked One and Wolf Boy protected them. How her mother had done small magics and made sachets and infusions for the people in town.

Abraham drew some of what she described. He couldn't see it, not like how he'd seen the past. But it was close enough that she was able to exclaim, "Yes! That's it!" when he sketched out her farm.

The roof was pitched wrong. "Are you sure that's it? Why is the roof so steep?" Abraham asked.

"So the snow will slide off more easily in the spring thaws," Erin told him.

While the farm and the land Erin had described in some ways resembled every other small farm, that roof was too different. He'd never seen a place like that around here.

She must be from far away.

When he'd finished, he noticed that she was yawning, and the boy's eyes were drooping.

Abraham very tore the sheet from his notebook and gave it to the girl.

"Thank you," she said, carefully folding it up and sticking it down the front of her dress. "I don't know if I'll be able to keep it, but it may help me get there. Or find someone who can send me there."

Abraham suspected that it was a small god who was making her travel from place to place, for some reason known only to that god. But he didn't say anything. He let the young people sleep and stayed awake through the night, watching carefully for anything stirring the woods around them, paying attention to every wind.

In the morning, Abraham started awake. He hadn't planned on sleeping. Something must have put him to sleep. How very strange.

But Erin was still there, curled up under Joey's spare blanket.

It wasn't until later that morning that they figured out that the drawing was gone.

# Twenty-Three

Angel stayed hidden in the trees, watching Erin, Joey, and Abraham go up the trail. She could follow them—and she might, later. For now, though, her charge was someone else's responsibility.

Angel remembered waking to the new world. She'd stood at one end of an altar, her brilliant wings spread wide. She knew that she was an angel of the LORD, though she had never actually talked with Him, or been in His presence.

The other angel, standing at the other end of the altar, hadn't woken. She was never certain why. Was it because the other angel was male? Had his marble not been as pure as hers? Had he not been carved correctly?

It was one of the mysteries of the LORD that Angel pondered frequently.

Angel had met other beings, like the Great Bear Man in Halifax, the snake ladies along the Nile, and the Dancing Ice Wind down in southern Chile. They all were tied to an area, though. Their calling from the LORD was to stay and protect the land, along with the people there.

It was a patchwork of bright spots at best, with many holes and pockets. And those holes were increasing. The *myst* was everywhere, now. All over the world, though Angel was infrequently called to places outside of the former Americas.

Angel had never had a territory, a plot of land, a mountain or a village that called to her. She'd been drawn to people. And not a town or village, or even a farm or family. Erin had been the only one the LORD had directed Angel to save more than once, the only person across the decades that Angel had had some kind of constant contact with.

Angel knew she wasn't saving souls—that was up to the LORD. She would save lives, though. Sometimes obviously, like with Erin. Sometimes in subtle ways that the person would never even know about, by turning the *myst* that was just beyond the next hill to the side, or sending the person down a second trail.

But most often in ways that Angel never understood. She'd approach a town and feel herself changing—growing old or young, male or female, magical or mundane. She would meet people there, in the village or town, talk with them about this or that, then leave again.

She never knew why she had to play these parts, what it was that she said that changed these people's lives or saved them, but she'd been doing it since the very first days of the *myst*.

Erin's need had been the greatest Angel had ever seen. Angel had saved Erin before the *myst* had swallowed her whole as it spilled across the road.

The *myst* hadn't paused, though. It had gone on to destroy Erin's entire village. She could never go back home. And Angel had no way of telling her. When Angel put Erin on the road and appeared before her, the girl couldn't see her.

That had happened to Angel before—she only appeared to those in need, and never as herself.

This time it made Angel inexpressibly sad. She'd wanted to talk with the girl.

Angel had initially placed Erin in the next village. She'd given her the clothing of that village so she'd fit in.

Angel hadn't realized that the village was a bad place. That the Elders there would consider Erin a witch and planned to kill her in a bizarre sacrifice that would *not* have pleased the LORD, no matter what those Elders claimed.

So Angel saved Erin a second time, the only time she'd ever been called to do that.

And yet, still the girl couldn't see her.

Then Angel got called to the place that had once been called Brazil. She just took Erin with her. It was easier than trying to check in with her.

But Erin had needed saving again. She couldn't stay in the new place. So Angel carried Erin with her. Tried to talk with her every night. Talked only with herself instead.

And so it went, for at least half a year. The LORD kept calling Angel to Erin. The girl wasn't settled yet.

When Erin started seeking out magicians, Angel tried placing her closer to them. But generally, she just dropped Erin close to the person she had to go save.

Erin didn't seem to appreciate the traveling. But Angel couldn't just drop her off. That was not the will of the LORD.

Plus, Erin was always seeking ways to go back to her home, and that was dangerous. Angel tried to warn her, again and again. But Erin could never hear her.

Where Joey and Abraham were going was also dangerous. But Angel was content to let Erin travel with them.

Maybe the LORD would call Angel to save Erin again. Though maybe it was time for Erin to save herself.

Angel still had the drawings of the magician Abraham, the pictures of Erin, that Angel could look at and remember the girl who had needed her so desperately but who had also defied her, cutting her hair and cursing the movement the LORD had forced upon her.

Angel whispered a blessing on the wind for Erin, then spread her white wings and flew inland, to the next person she must save.

# Twenty-Four

Basad looked at the plans spread out across the table in the tavern. It was a rough sketch of the town and their defenses. The barricades to the south. The tinder piles, well-disguised and ready to explode with a single spark. The number of men and women available to fight. The numbers of families who had fled.

Once again, Basad didn't know if he should curse Abraham or thank him for warning his town about the coming horde.

Fields went untended, the fall harvest rotting. *Myst* crept in anywhere they didn't fight it, daily. Some of the houses would have to stay abandoned, even if the families came back.

No one had seen the horde. There was no news from the south. None the scouts Basad had sent out had returned.

Were they all dead? Turned by the horde? Would they come back *wyrd* and ready to fight their own families?

The two nearby magicians had promised to come when the horde arrived. They wouldn't be enough—not if every man in the horde was magical.

Maybe the Horned One and Chikee Kowa would come as well. Maybe if they all fought together they'd have a chance.

Maybe the great cities would all rise back up, fresh and new, and the great fall would be erased as well.

Basar sighed. There wasn't much more he could do, here, with his maps and his plans. He straightened up, stretching his hands over his head. He should sleep, if he could. Amy, the tavern owner, had laid down a pile of straw and some blankets in the corner so Basar could sleep there.

Basar didn't need a mirror to know that even his dark skin could no longer hide the black circles under his eyes. Of course, now that he admitted to being tired, his exhaustion slammed into him. He stumbled over to the corner and knelt down.

Basar remembered the *mantras* his mother and great-grandmother had taught him, singing prayers to Brahma, the one. How they'd changed even in his lifetime to include the Horned One.

He merely mumbled one recitation of the Gonda mantra and collapsed, settling in for a dark sleep.

He'd barely closed his eyes when Serge came racing in.

"They're coming."

Basar struggled to rise, adrenaline chasing away his calm. "How close?"

"Less than an hour away," Serge said. "They hid their approach."

Basar swore. They had scouts several days out, and a system that was supposed to warn the town two or three days in advance.

He ran behind Serge to the barrier.

Echoes of eerie calls drifted on the winds, raising all the hair on Basar's neck. It sounded like the growl of some great machine the ancestors would have built. *Myst* floated nearby, like a sickly web, ready to pounce once they turned their backs.

Basar found more prayers on his lips, a useless prayer for peace.

How could there be peace with an enemy who couldn't be reasoned with, who was no longer human?

But Basar prayed on, even as the horde broke across the wooden barrier like an ocean wave, piling one body on top of another to reach the top and come over, fighting and killing and turning every man and woman they touched.

# Twenty-Five

Joey couldn't help but gasp as they cleared the ridge.

"Boeing Field," Abraham announced. "Where they used to make airplanes. And fly them."

Down below, huge hulks of machinery sat rusting on long concrete strips. Was that a plane? The wings had broken off a long, skinny body.

How had they survived so long? All the cars had rusted away, long ago, when people stopped caring about them, when they'd realized the cars would never run again. Possibly some of the boulders they'd passed near the road had once been cars.

Gently rolling hills sloped between the edge of the cliff and the field, covered in clover. The slope flattened at one, wide point. Had that been the highway? Why wasn't it covered in trees, like most of the highways? What had been maintaining it?

Then Joey gasped again. Seattle stood just to the north. Tall, dark buildings rising out of the water, like huge iron trees. Abraham had shown Joey drawings of what Seattle had once looked like. It wasn't as crowded—many of the buildings had collapsed.

What would it be like to take a boat through the canals between the buildings there? Would either Ocean or the Great Inland Sea permit it?

"Why is it so clear through here?" Joey asked. Abraham had warned them that the woods would have grown up all around Seattle, and chances were, they'd never have a clear view.

And why was Boeing Field so open? The planes merely rusted, and not completely covered?

"I don't know," Abraham said. "Except…There."

A man walked out on Boeing field. Except it couldn't have been just a man. Not if Joey could see him from this distance. His head was even with the tops of the rusting planes on the field.

"Who is that?" Erin asked, curious.

"Not a who," Abraham said. "A what."

The man pulled back the roof of one of the planes and pulled out something that he then attached to his own arm.

His mechanical arm.

It looked like a lance that extended past his hand. Then he turned and marched north.

"Wow," Joey said. Then he realized what he'd just said and how stupid it had sounded. He glanced at Erin, but she didn't seem to notice.

Abraham got out his spyglass and looked down at the field.

Joey still felt ashamed that he'd first thought the spyglass was a stick. But he'd never seen one before. And it kind of looked like a well-polished stick, about the length of a man's arm, long and smooth.

"Ah," Abraham said after a moment, handing the spyglass to Joey.

Joey carefully took the spyglass and put his right eye, while remembering to close his left. Just north of the field lapped the Great Inland Sea. It amazed him at how close it looked now.

And it wasn't magic. It was merely *optics*, as Abraham had explained to Joey, something the ancients had known all about.

Then Joey saw the man. He was only partially human—his face looked human, and his left arm, and his torso.

The rest all appeared to be made out of many metal blocks welded together.

Though Joey couldn't hear what the man was saying from this distance, he could read his actions. The man yelled, roaring at the water, stabbing it with his lance.

The water rolled back slowly.

There was no barricade to keep it back. No wall or dam.

Just the will of the mechanical man, who ran Boeing field.

Joey handed the spyglass to Erin, who gave a low whistle as she looked. "Don't think those two get along at all," she said as she handed the spyglass back to Abraham.

"No, I wouldn't imagine so," Abraham said. "I knew that Ocean had found her voice after the rifts. I hadn't imagined that the Great Inland Sea would as well."

Joey shrugged. He had only heard about the sea from Billy the bard. He was relieved that Billy had been right.

"What would you have done if Joey hadn't been right about the sea?" Erin asked.

Joey froze. He knew better than to ask that kind of question. While Abraham was more human than other magician's Joey had met, particularly on this trip, Abraham was still a magician.

"Drown him there," Abraham said without hesitation. "Come on. We won't get to the shore tonight, but maybe, if we can follow the clear roads, we'll get there in a couple days."

Abraham started to carefully navigate down the cliff face, clutching one boulder, then doing a controlled slide to the next. When he looked up at Joey, he gave a broad wink.

Was Abraham only fooling about drowning him? Joey wasn't sure. He wasn't surprised at all by Abraham's answer. The magician excelled at being practical. He'd left Joey and Erin behind more than once on their journey, frustrated with their pace. They'd find him the next day, farther up the trail, after he'd taken a side-route to another town, warning them of the horde.

Joey and Erin helped each other down the rocky cliff. Joey wasn't surprised that when he dug his fingers into the turf that there was rust underneath. They had been cars here, once.

Joey was careful to keep his help friendly, like a brother. He tried to only be friendly with Erin, to never presume that she would be interested in more. No girl would ever want him—all magicians lived alone.

He'd never have a wife or a family.

The city of Seattle loomed ahead of them, across the clover plain. The sea seeped all around it, dark and still. Marshes made up the edges, islands of floating greenery. Tall towers loomed above the water. Birds flew in and out of the blackened squares—had they once been windows? One of the buildings to the left still had a pointed roof, like a cap. Most were flat-roofed, though. To the right, where the hills started and the water ended, piled *myst* and darkness.

"What will you say when you get there?" Erin asked.

She'd asked that before. Joey still had no idea how he was going to ask his question of the Great Inland Sea and not get himself killed. He shrugged.

He knew that Abraham would ask the sea about the horde, how to stop it. That was all he cared about.

It surprised Joey how much Abraham cared about stopping the horde. Was he scared of it? Or had it done something personal to him?

Joey still wanted to ask about the blue-dragon-egg rocks and how to get the winter witch to hatch them.

He believed the two questions were related.

He hoped the Great Inland Sea thought so as well.

Though the night had been wet and cold (and if Joey was honest, kind of miserable), morning dawned clear and cool. Tall herons stalked the nearby marsh islands of the Great Inland Sea. Seagulls wheeled above the calm waters to the west, complaining about the lack of easy fish.

The previous night, Abraham had speared three large dusky, silver-gray perch for their dinner. He'd eaten that night—maybe he needed the energy for the coming day? Or maybe he'd just wanted to sit with Joey and Erin, almost like a normal person, telling stories of his past as they sat around the fire and the sky lit up with a million stars?

To the west of their camp, the Great Inland Sea opened up, with a great expanse of water between the land and the snow-peaked mountains against the horizon. Abraham said that there used to be islands visible from the Seattle shore. Not any longer—the water had swallowed them all.

Directly north was the remains of the city itself. Joey could now see the vines that covered the buildings, growing out of the water and encasing them like a lover's embrace. Flocks of birds dived from the blackened windows down to the sea, hunting fish. Were the birds controlled by the *myst*? It was impossible to know at this distance.

To the east lay hills entrapped in *myst*. Neighborhoods that used to be full of houses and people were displaced by trees and darkness.

The *myst* crouched at the shores of the water, like a cat waiting to pounce. Winds from the sea kept it at bay.

If the horde reached here, what would it do? Would it disturb the water enough to break its hold on the city? Would it poison the fish and the waters?

Abraham stood next to the shore, hands behind his back, contemplating the water.

Joey went and stood beside him, with Erin at his side.

Abraham seemed to be humming. Joey looked anxiously at him, then at Erin, who just shrugged.

Who knew what a magician would do?

Finally, Abraham turned to Joey. "I've tried talking to the Great Inland Sea. She's aware that we're here, that we have questions. However, I'm not sure she'll deal with me. You'll have to do it."

"How?" Joey asked.

Abraham opened his mouth, then closed it again. "Honestly, I'm not sure. I thought I would know when I got here. But I don't. You'll have to figure it out yourself."

*Great.* Joey sighed, exasperated, as Abraham walked back to their camp.

"Any suggestions?" Joey asked Erin.

"How badly do you want this?" Erin asked seriously. "Truly want to know?" Then she turned and walked away.

She wanted to go back home, to her family, her village at the foot of the mountains. She wanted it badly enough to pester every person they met, ask the magicians of every town they went to warn, about how to go back. She was constantly planning how to return there.

Another reason why Joey could never do more than admire her from afar. She had her path. He had his.

What he didn't have was an answer to her question. How much did he want the blue-dragon-egg rocks to turn into actual dragons? What would that mean? Would it save his town? His family? The farm? Their crops?

Joey sat down on a rock on the edge of the marsh. Wind blew the tall, golden reeds. Frogs sang with deep voices about the coming winter. Ducks flew overhead in a perfect V, heading south. Dandelion seeds danced on the wind, reminding Joey of the witches.

He'd never dreamed of dragons, unlike his older brother. But he could see it, now. The awakening of a great dragon. The tower, long and slim, morphing into the neck of a dragon. Growing the head, the walls at the bottom changing into legs and wings.

The scales of the dragon would be all the colors of the rocks, from dark blue to almost whitish-gray. It would breathe the same blue flames that Joey could call up, belching them into the sky, roaring at the *myst* and then taking off, flying at it. Destroying great swaths of it from the air.

Then burning the horde. All those men who had gone *wyrd*. Like Max. Or maybe the flames could turn them sane again.

Joey shivered, waking up from his daydream. The sun was far to the west. He'd been there for a long while, daydreaming about the dragon rocks and the tower.

Joey found his attention turning to the north.

A young woman stood on the waters.

Joey didn't feel any surprise or fear—just wonder.

She had golden and blue scales all over her skin. Her eyes were pink and white and blue. Not human at all. They faced to the side, like a fish's. She didn't have hair. Her head was shaped like a rosebud. At the very top of her skull, the tips of the flower were green and opened slightly.

She didn't speak as she walked across the water to Joey.

The woman sat down next to Joey and sighed. Joey tried to speak, but found he couldn't, not in this place.

Was this the Great Inland Sea? Her avatar?

A gentle questioning washed over Joey. The very air felt as though it held question marks. The wind stilled, holding its breath, waiting for answers.

Joey put all his hope, all his fervent wishing, into showing this woman the blue-dragon-egg rocks. How the winter witches danced on the cool winter winds and spread their glittering frost. How someday the rocks would hatch into something like dragons.

The woman nodded. Confusion and images poured from her.

She'd never heard of the blue-dragon-rock eggs. They weren't in any of the pages and pages of books she'd absorbed, dissolving the words in her waves. None of the people she'd absorbed had any idea. She showed him how she'd drained them, their thoughts and ideas and magic sluiced off them with her waters.

Joey tried to hide the horror he felt as the terror of all those people dying came over him.

The air was full of questioning again. Why would he care about people he'd never met?

Joey answered with the first thought that came to his head. Because he was human, and not a magician. Not yet.

Suddenly, the images from the woman changed.

Joey saw his own face being drowned, his thoughts dissolved and shared by the sea.

It wasn't an absolute prediction of the future. The image was tinged with curiosity.

Why should she let him live?

Despair flooded Joey. All his fears multiplied. The horde was coming. The land would soon be covered in *myst*. His family would be killed, or worse, turned *wyrd* and become part of the army.

Joey fought to find hope. The blue flames he carried, deep within him: He'd denied them his entire life. But he wanted, *needed* to experience them fully, at least once.

Joey's despair receded.

The emotions hadn't all been from him. She'd been testing him.

The woman nodded. Joey had something unique to do. She would let him live.

Joey thanked the sea as best he could, trying to find and feel all the gratitude he could.

The woman continued to sit there, beside him, looking out over the water.

Joey dared ask about the horde. Showed her the image of Max, then multiplied tenfold. How could they be defeated? He extended the image through the land he'd passed through, how the horde would reach the sea at some point.

The woman shuddered, then shrugged. The Sound had survived Man, both the rise and the fall of him. She would survive both the rise and the fall of the *myst* as well.

Joey wasn't sure about that, but he didn't know how to convince the Great Inland Sea of the danger. It seemed inconceivable that anything could hurt her, though even she knew the *myst* would try.

When the woman walked back into the sea Joey continued to sit there, still locked in place by the sea's soothing swishing sound. It wasn't until a wave came and splashed his feet that Joey started and came back to himself.

It was still late afternoon. The water looked as though it was on fire from the orange beams cast by the sun.

For a terrible moment, Joey thought he saw the water on fire, the *myst* and the horde cackling gleefully on the shore, the Great Inland Sea unable to fight back.

The image passed, though. Crushing disappointment weighed Joey down.

Had he made this journey for nothing?

They'd warned many towns, yes, but they had no new knowledge about fighting the horde.

No clue as to how to hatch the blue-dragon-egg rocks.
Another bad winter was coming.
And the *myst* was gaining power everywhere.

# Twenty-Six

Carl grabbed the fresh bread with both hands and ravenously tore into it. His jaw clicked as he chewed. The *myst* hadn't bothered to fix his face. He knew it could. Maybe it was to keep him different than all the rest.

Ima ate beside him, though without his gusto. Maybe she was more like the others in the horde, and didn't need food. They lived on *myst* and magic.

Carl knew this made the horde unstoppable. An army marched on its stomach. As long as there was enough *myst*, they would be able to keep marching on.

Jim didn't need any food. Or even any rest.

Carl still did, though. He knew that ironically, by letting him eat, Jim was suppressing Carl's ability to sway him. With hunger as a weapon, Carl could get Jim to turn away, let someone join the horde instead of being killed.

The *myst* only fed Jim. And Carl's body. Not Little Carl, still buried deep inside.

Ima didn't have the problems that Carl did. She wasn't *wyrd* like the others. She was more like him, with thoughts and plans and dreams. She had more words, too. Sometimes, when a town was efficiently protected behind locked gates, he'd send her to talk with the townspeople, to reason with them. To trick them into letting her in.

It had only worked once. But it had meant fewer losses. Fewer men to heal.

The *myst* cured simple wounds, like being stabbed by a knife. A broken bone meant death, usually. And at least one of the towns had been armed with swords. They'd lost many men there, decapitated, though they weren't the zombies the town had prepared for.

Carl reached for the apples, next. Sweet juices dribbled down his chin. The fall harvest had been good here. He longed for the sweet pulp of a pumpkin, but Jim would never let him near a flame, and wouldn't wait around long enough for it to be cooked.

So Carl made do with whatever food he could scavenge before they burned the place to the ground.

That was Ima's specialty. She called up flames from everywhere—deep in the house as well as lines burned far underground. When she wasn't careful, she'd set men on fire as well.

She didn't seem to care.

At least she cared about what happened to her. When Jim had tried to do things to her, she'd called up the flames. Only the *myst* had saved him. Carl had cheered her on, despite how the fire had hurt.

Jim was nice to Ima now. Trying to get on her good side. Like letting her eat. Trying to get her to trust him. To let her guard down.

Even Carl knew that was impossible. Ima was too careful.

Jim was doomed. As were all the towns north of them. And the whole world.

# Twenty-Seven

Abraham's hand blurred across the page, trying to capture the images pouring over him. The iron and wood gate stretching across the trade road. The debris—apple barrels, dug-out rusted machinery, sharpened wooden pikes—bulging out along both sides, trying to make the blockage bigger.

The horde—faceless, really, mainly just heads with huge eyes—pouring over the gate. The bodies piling up, blunting the spikes. The desperate townspeople, fighting with lances and spears. Keeping the enemy at arm's length.

Overwhelmed. The town burning.

Abraham became aware of the two young people staring at him with horror. Why? Had he changed?

Then he realized it wasn't him. It was his drawings. The tale of war he told.

It had happened in the past. Not the far past, but recent.

And would happen again. Soon.

"How do you see such things?" Joey asked when Abraham's hand finally slowed. Stopped.

Abraham carefully closed his sketch book and put it away. Stretched his cramped fingers, encouraging warmth to flow back through them.

Joey's question still hung in the air. "Magic," Abraham finally responded. His magic had always come to him that way.

He'd never spent any time with other magicians. He didn't know how their magic came. He supposed Joey's would come with flames. That he'd feel flames deep inside him.

Abraham would always find his magic in pictures, images of what he wanted to do, then doing it. As long as he could see it, clearly behold what he wanted in his mind, he could do it.

"Will we get back in time?" Joey asked.

Abraham didn't know how to answer that. In time for what? Winter was coming. Trees held more branches than leaves.

"Before the horde reaches Lakeland," Erin clarified.

"I don't know," Abraham said. There was no way for him to know, not without rushing back to the town to see.

"What will you do when we get there?" Abraham asked Joey, curious. He knew the boy considered the trip a personal failure. He'd learned along the way, however. He'd seen the great ruins of Seattle. Talked with the Great Inland Sea, and survived.

Abraham had warned many towns of the coming horde. They would have time to prepare. To flee.

He didn't consider their trip a failure at all.

"I don't know," Joey said. He looked off into the darkness, beyond the single light of their campfire. "Talk with the winter witch. She's got to be here, by now. Make her see."

Abraham nodded and didn't reply. He'd never had any luck talking with Crested Cook. The small gods had their own agenda, and it rarely coincided with what man wanted. They were just lucky that the small gods hated the *myst*.

# Twenty-Eight

Joey pushed back from the dining-room table. "No, Ma, I can't eat another bite," he told her as she came up, bearing another slice of apple pie.

The whole family was there for his—*their*—return. The rest of the town still made frantic preparations for the coming horde, merely a day away, if the reports were accurate.

But Joey's family had been excused to welcome him home.

He knew they hoped he'd have some good news.

Abraham hadn't stayed, and Joey was just as glad. He'd gotten used to the magician and his strange ways, but Abraham would have made everyone else uncomfortable.

Erin had nowhere else to go. Ma welcomed her like a daughter. It was strange to see Erin in something other than her plain brown robe, but once they got inside, she gladly shed it in exchange for warm, brown-wool pants, an unbleached cotton shirt and a leather vest. She kept her knife with her—Joey assumed it was habit, as much as anything else. She looked different than everyone else at the table, with her strangely cut hair, her teasing smile, the secrets that still haunted her eyes.

Joey had gladly changed out of his travel-stained clothes into fresh pants and shirt. The fire in the fireplace kept the house toasty and warm.

The haunted corner was more quiet, shrouded by a curtain that had been drenched in salt water and left to dry.

He'd talked and talked and talked, all the way through dinner, shoving as much of Ma's good cooking into his mouth as he could between answering questions. Of the towns he'd seen. The hulking remains of Seattle. The mechanical god that protected Boeing field. The Great Inland Sea.

Finally, though, after the tea had been served, Da asked, "So what can we do about the horde?"

Joey sighed and played with his cup. "The Great Inland Sea had no answers. She wasn't concerned. She'd survived man. She felt she'd survive the *myst*. She didn't have any reason to help us."

Everyone at the table seemed to deflate at that.

"Most of the town has fled," Da admitted. "There will be some resistance, some men who will fight. Large barriers that have been built along the road."

"And the blue-dragon-egg rocks?" Nathan asked, the littlest cousin. "Did you ask about those?"

"I did," Joey said. "They were the reason the Great Inland Sea let me live," he lied. "She'd never seen anything about them. Had never heard of them."

Joey looked at Erin, who nodded. He had to tell them the rest of his plan. He stood up from the table. "Tonight, I'm spending the night on the tower. I'm going to make the winter witch hatch the eggs."

Stunned silence greeted him.

"No," Ma said quietly. "You'll not throw your life away."

Da started to say something. Ma overrode him. "I know, I know. The horde is merely a day away. But you're young. You can still run."

"I'm not running, Ma," Joey said. "I need to stay here. Fight. Get the winter witch to hatch the dragons. Or the world is doomed."

"Why will the witch listen to you?" Nathan asked reasonably.

"Because I'll destroy the tower if she doesn't," Joey told them.

"How?" Da asked, incredulous.

With a deep sigh, Joey called up the blue fire. It was easier, now. Frighteningly easy. The flames danced along his fingertips.

The haunted corner sniggered to itself.

Joey doused the fire and looked around the table. "I will tear the tower down, stone by stone, to get her to talk with me. To do my will. There's no other way. We all know the witches love the tower. They rest on it nightly. Tonight will be the last night."

"It was Brendon's will that it be maintained," Da said softly.

"I know. Our ancestors wanted that tower to grow. But did it ever occur to you why?" Joey asked. "The taller it was, the more rocks we had, the more *dragons* we'll have."

"Do you really think you can get the winter witch to hatch the blue-dragon-egg rocks?" the youngest cousin asked.

"I must," Joey told her simply. Otherwise they'd all be dead when the horde arrived.

Joey stood at the base of the tower. The night had come quickly. He was grateful for the extra wool coat that Da had given him, along with the warm scarf.

He hadn't taken the mittens Mom had offered. They'd get in the way.

Stars shone down from a deeply black sky. Cold winds nipped at his ears and cheeks. Just beyond the field stood the first grove of trees. The *myst* hung from the dark branches like sickly snow. Strange noises carried on the wind, like insane babies crying.

The ladders had all been put away for the winter. Joey still easily climbed the tower, the uneven rocks making good handholds and footholds. As a kid, he and his cousins had had races to see who could get to the top first.

It was colder on the highest platform. Joey could see all the surrounding fields up to the edges of the trees, and beyond some of those, even.

Joey didn't see the winter witch. Didn't know where she was. How to call her.

He picked up one of the top rocks that hadn't been cemented into the tower yet. Deep inside the rock he felt…something. He'd always known which was a blue-dragon-egg-rock, without ever having to pick it up or scrape at the surface.

They were his prize. Something he'd always coveted, cherishing when he found one previously undiscovered in a field and had carried it home.

The blue flames came quickly. The wind stirred. Joey knew the *myst* was watching. It would try to speak with him, soon.

Joey cast his flame on the rock, baking it.

It wasn't enough.

Joey heated the rock hotter, willing it to shatter.

The rock stayed stubbornly in one piece.

Frustrated, Joey hurled the rock against the platform.

It didn't shatter.

"Ahhhhhrrrrr!" Joey screamed. All his anger and frustration and fear boiled up. He made a chopping motion with his hand as he smote the rock with flames.

It split in two.

Magic leaped up inside Joey. He could feel it, now. Burning just below the surface of his skin.

He remembered the stories he'd heard about other magicians. How it was like ice or water.

The way Joey found his magic was through fire.

He saw the path clearly, now. How he could turn away from the heat. Let it die in the cold morning, be overrun by the horde.

Or he could bake it into his bones. Encourage his blood to bubble and boil.

He'd change. Lose his family. His home.

He didn't have a choice.

Burning with fury, Joey smote another rock. And another.

His sight changed. He saw more. The world was brighter. More alive.

When he broke the next rock, he saw the magic spark in the center of it ignite briefly, then die.

"Come deal with me," Joey dared the winter witch as he broke another rock. "Come sing to me. Now."

Before he reduced the tower to rubble and there was nothing left to hatch.

# Twenty-Nine

Odlen danced in meadow, spreading her frost in a big circle as she swirled. The night was so pretty! Stars shone down from a clear sky. *Myst* gathered in the trees, but she didn't care about that. It was her time to dance. The winds were just right, not too cold, not too hot. They fed her.

And Odlen needed to feed.

Her stupid sister Spira had barely fed them at all! Odlen wondered what she'd been doing. There were plenty of leaves around. Why hadn't Spira danced with them more?

Now it was up to her to make it all up. *She* wouldn't leave her sisters in a lurch.

Later that night, she'd go to the house, too. The boy had returned. Maybe he'd talk with her now, as his predecessors had talked with her sisters.

Singing quietly, Odlen circled the clearing again. There was *myst* somewhere. Causing trouble. Maybe she could gather enough power to herself that she could bind it with frost, the way her summer sisters bound it with sunlight.

No, no, that would take too much energy. And Odlen needed it all for herself if she was to survive the colder months, the times when it grew dark and the frost pinched the remains of her toes, the vestiges that dangled at the ends of her string-like legs.

What was that *myst* doing? Odlen felt unsettled. It wasn't the horde. That was to the south. No, this was north. With the family.

Worried, Odlen left her meadow and floated up above the trees.

It wasn't as if the boy would talk with her. But she still felt the need to see what was going on.

Odlen was horrified at what the boy had done. Her tower! The place that the family had built for her! He was destroying it!

He stopped, though, when she arrived.

Then he spoke directly to her!

"We need your help," he said.

Odlen nodded. She, or at least her sisters, had heard it all before.

"The horde is coming. You've seen it."

Odlen didn't nod. Not that time. She didn't want to admit that it was breathing down her neck. That her lands were about to be violated. Couldn't the boy understand? This was why she had to get back to dancing with the frost.

So she might survive the attack.

"We need the dragons," the boy said. "Or the horde will destroy us all."

Odlen sighed. She knew that there was something that she was supposed to do with the rocks. She'd always known. So had all her sisters.

But to do what the boy asked…would be like facing the horde all alone. She wouldn't survive.

The boy must have seen her hesitation. He reached for another rock, one of the stronger ones, and set it on fire. "You might live through the attack if the tower stays standing," he told her. "But I'll make sure it's gone if you turn away now. You *must* help us."

Why was it always the winter witch who had to make these hard choices? Couldn't she just dance, for one more day?

But the time of dancing had ended. Just as her sisters had always known it would.

"Now," Joey instructed her.

With a sigh, Odlen flew closer to the tower, her spirits dropping further. She wouldn't survive. She just knew it. Chances were, she would be the last of the witches, the very last of her line.

If she wasn't, if she somehow miraculously survived, maybe one of her sisters would remember her someday, and honor the sacrifice that she made.

She spread her fingers wide and frosted the outer rocks, the very top of the tower, blessing them with her magic, her true magic.

"Thank you. Thank you," came the whispered words.

Odlen didn't take the time to curtsey. It was only her right to get his thanks.

She flew down to the base of the tower, still casting her frost. Then she flew up one side, and around again.

The tower turned white, sparkling in the dark night.

Exhausted, Olden flew back to the top. It wasn't enough. Just spending her magic wasn't ever going to be enough.

*Remember me*, she whispered, her words carried on the wind from the tower to the house. They would all dream of her that night, and the sisters who had come before her.

Would it be enough? She would never know.

Odlen darted up toward the sky. Better to make this quick.

Then she plunged down, folding her dandelion skirts around her, plummeting into the hollow center of the tower.

The rocks reached for her, scraped off pieces of her as she fell, whittling her down, until she was merely a white stick, still falling, dropping down onto the ground at the very base of the tower. Giving away every piece of her until there was almost nothing left.

Just a smidgen remained as she hit the rock at the bottom, burning the very last of her up, turning it red.

Using all her magic would never have been enough.

The dragons needed every part of her, including her life.

# Thirty

Joey watched, astonished, as the winter witch finally did what he'd asked. The frost she'd spread had been pretty.

But even he could tell it wasn't enough.

Fear had leaped high in Joey's chest when the white witch had flown up, high into the sky. She wasn't flying` away, was she?

Then she streaked like a falling star, aiming for the opening of the tower, disappearing deep within.

Sorrow struck Joey then. He knew what she was doing. She was giving herself, all her magic and her life, to hatch the dragons.

Would there ever be more witches? Or was she the last of her line?

Joey wiped the cold tears from his eyes as the light faded. The tower rocks turned brown and gray again.

The life inside the rocks had quickened. They were different. He could tell that.

But the sacrifice of the winter witch hadn't been enough.

Somehow, Joey had always known it would be his turn next.

Maybe if they'd had time, the rocks would have hatched in the summer sun.

They were out of time.

Joey copied the stance of the winter witch, spread his hands wide, then threw his flame onto the rocks, heating them.

The magic ate away at Joey's soul as he poured everything onto the rocks. He was caught up in the beauty of the flame. But his family was now as far away from him as the distant city of Seattle.

Even Erin meant little to him now.

Joey circled the tower, casting as much flame as he knew how. It roared out of him, heating the rocks. He poured all of his soul into it. The rock *must* hatch. He let go of his anger, directing it too, into the flames, burning himself free of that emotion as well.

Slowly, Joey made his way to the ground. It felt different under his feet. As a farmer, the ground had always been a welcome, steady force to push against. Joey had never thought about it before, had always just known it was there.

Now, it felt dead.

The blue flames that licked the tower rocks grew smaller and fainter, until they died.

What had gone wrong? Did Joey need to give more of himself, as the witch had?

Joey was aware that before, he would have felt despair that he'd failed. Now, he felt a faint curiosity. Had he done something wrong? Was it not enough? He'd sacrificed all his feeling, all his emotion. His anger, his love, even his family.

But none of the dragons had hatched.

He was glad he felt almost nothing, or the despair would have been crushing.

Curious, Joey reached out to touch the tower. Was it still warm?

The rocks under his hand trembled.

# Thirty-One

Erin watched with the rest of Joey's family from the windows of the farm house. They'd included her easily enough, like a cousin. The clothes they'd given her felt familiar, scented with lavender and cedar to keep the spiders and the moths out. It felt good to finally wear regular pants and shirts again.

She wasn't sure if the being (and Abraham had been convinced it had been a small god) had left her behind for good. She'd hoped so.

That she'd been put there to be with Joey and Abraham for a reason.

Joey was on his way to becoming a magician. And Erin was planning on being there to help. No matter how strange he grew. He'd always be like Abraham, she suspected, more human than the rest.

Joey's mom brought Erin to stand beside her, so she could see better.

Her own mother—was she even alive? Erin had no idea. But Erin wanted to think that her mom would be just as kind if her brother brought home a stranger.

The night pressed in against the glass window, bringing a chill to the room. Erin pulled a borrowed shawl tighter over her shoulders as the first spark of flame sliced open one of the rocks.

Everyone in the room gasped. "How can he destroy them?" Joey's mother asked.

"Because he has to," Erin gently reminded her. "To get the attention of the winter witch." She didn't dare tell the family that it had been her idea.

Joey had initially acted the same way as the rest of his family, horrified at committing such a sacrilege.

But Abraham had agreed. It was probably the only way to get the attention of the winter witch.

Erin's breath caught when the winter witch flew up. She was beautiful, despite her pointed nose and chin, her sharp teeth and claws. Her skin glowed like fresh snow in the moonlight. Her skirt blossomed under her like a dandelion gone to seed. Mere strings hung down under the skirt. Had they been legs at one point? The witch did look vaguely human, at least from the waist up.

Joey and the winter witch talked for a while. What had they said? Was Joey arguing with her? Or merely showing her the inevitable?

Erin released a breath she hadn't known she was holding when the winter witch started coating the tower in frost. While the frost pattern crystalizing over the stones was a familiar sight, like what she'd seen on mountain rocks during the winter, it was still breathtaking. She suddenly wished that Abraham was there, so that he could capture the image in a picture.

No one expected the winter witch to fall like a star into the tower, disappearing into its depths. The rocks seemed to freeze, then, the whiteness growing as the light of the winter witch descended.

But it hadn't been enough. The white glow faded.

The eggs wouldn't hatch.

"No, no," Joey's mother said. She turned away, Joey's father coming to hold her as she cried.

The disappointment that filled the room made it hard to breathe.

Would the family run? Run before the coming horde?

Or would the disappointment drag them down, make them fight and die when the horde arrived?

What had gone wrong? Why hadn't the witch's magic been enough?

"Maybe they'll hatch come spring," Nathan, the youngest said.

The boy didn't understand how desperate their need was. There was no spring, not for them.

Joey needed to do something more.

Erin knew Joey resisted his magic. He wanted to stay normal. Human.

But to save them, he would have to sacrifice his connection with them, like the good boy he was.

It made her more determined than ever to stay with him.

The flames didn't surprise Erin. She'd seen him use them before.

The rest of the family seemed shocked though.

"He has to," Erin said softly.

They nodded, but Erin knew they didn't understand what the cost would be.

They'd find out soon enough.

When Joey touched ground, the eggs still hadn't hatched. He put his hand against the rocks, then jumped back, startled.

The tower started to shake.

"We need to go help him," Erin said as the shaking grew more violent.

"How?" Joey's mother asked.

"There's *myst* outside," Joey's father said.

"And so is your son. About to give birth to a hundred dragons. Or more," Erin told him as she hurried out of the room.

Joey's oldest brother raced ahead of her to the door. He smeared the salt and chalk sigil with a deliberate swipe, then looked up. "Ready?" he asked.

Erin nodded. She didn't know who would race outside with her. It didn't matter. She had to be there. Had to help.

Nathan the youngest cousin opened the door and Erin, Joey's father, and Joey's sister all darted outside. The door slammed immediately after them. Erin knew they'd be frantically redrawing the sigil and pouring the salt, racing to keep the house secure from the *myst*.

Erin looked around carefully. She didn't see any *myst* nearby. Didn't hear it, either. She suspected that it was distracted by what was happening at the tower.

She was still careful, though, running across the yard, through the gate, to the tower. But no beasts lay hidden in the shadows, ready to claw at her. No screaming ghosts suddenly jumped out.

Joey didn't seem to know what to do. He stood with his golden eyes watching the tower, trying to take it all in.

"Is there any place we should start?" Erin asked Joey as they came up.

"Start?" Joey asked, confused.

"Haven't you ever seen a chick hatch?" Erin asked, frustrated. Men. They knew so little.

"That's a good theory," Joey said. "I will follow your lead."

He could have been talking about an afternoon snack, and not the birth of dragons, the blue-dragon-egg rocks that had meant enough to him to go all the way to the Great Inland Sea.

Erin couldn't mourn the loss of Joey's humanity right now, though.

She pulled at one of the smaller eggs along the bottom of the tower. "Here," she said, thrusting it at Joey's dad. "Go put this on one side."

Erin collected together the eggs that seemed warmest, that were rocking the hardest. They could hatch on their own.

The others she collected into a small pile, wrapping them with her shawl, trying to keep them warmer. "Can you set a fire here?" she asked.

Joey nodded. "Here." He set blue flames burning next to the shawl. "But what about the ones up there?" he asked.

"They'll just have to hatch up there," Erin said. "I hope they're born fliers."

"I can bring them down," Joey said calmly.

"Yes, please," Erin told him. "Quickly."

Joey removed about three feet of stones from the top of the tower. The others sorted them quickly, as soon as a rock touched the ground, either placing them closer to the flames to keep them warm, or else putting them in the other pile, separate, so they could hatch on their own.

Suddenly, a great *crack* filled the quiet night.

They all raced around to the far side of the tower.

A rock about two stories up had hatched. In the hole in the wall crouched a tiny lizard-looking creature. It had bright blue scales and golden eyes.

Erin gasped. So did Joey's dad and sister.

"You did it," Joey's dad said. "You did it."

"I couldn't have done it alone," Joey said. "The winter witch…she gave her life."

Erin looked at Joey. He sounded so sad. Almost human.

The dragon gave a tiny cackle, like a baby goose. Then it launched itself out of the tower.

Straight for the far woods and the *myst*.

"The *myst* will kill it," Joey announced. "It should have waited until it was bigger."

"How fast will they grow?" Erin asked. How long did they have to wait until the dragons could fight the *myst*? They didn't have time!

"I don't know," Joey said. He shrugged. "Fast, I think."

"Then we need to stop the others," Erin said firmly. "Joey, can you contain them?"

"No," he said slowly, drawing the word out and shaking his head. "They'd burn down a fence. Or fly over it. But maybe…" Joey looked back at the *myst* over near the trees. "Maybe I can keep them here."

Joey used his magic to scoop out a handful of dirt, then another, digging a quick hole. When it was about two feet deep and three feet wide he put both hands over it.

*Myst* filled the small hole, deadly and white. Tendrils trailed over the edges.

"How did you do that?" Erin asked horrified. "Can all magicians do that?" No wonder magicians weren't trusted! Not if they were that close to the *myst*.

"Yes," Joey said. "And no. They can all call it. Not many can contain it. It's too hard to do it for long. Luckily, it won't be just me."

Another dragon hatchling gave a crackling call, landing on the edge of the hole. It stuck its nose into the *myst*, sucking at it, like a newborn suckling.

"Why does it eat the *myst*?" Joey's dad asked, awe and terror filling his voice.

"The magic. It's sucking the magic away," Joey answered. "It isn't the *myst*. It's the magic inside the *myst*. If there wasn't *myst*, it would wait for me to cast magic, so it could absorb that."

The hatchling belched blue flame as it pulled back. It had already grown noticeably larger, almost the length of a man's arm, now.

More hatchlings joined around the edge of the *myst*-filled hole. Joey kept filling and refilling the hole with *myst*, giving the dragons their first taste. Joey's dad worked with him, making sure that every newborn got at least a few sips.

Hundreds of dragons piled up, mewling and cracking, growing at an astonishing rate.

"What are we going to do with all these dragons?" Erin asked as she stumbled back, exhausted from shifting rocks and hatchlings around all night. The sun had just broken over the horizon.

"Attack the horde," Joey told her calmly.

"They're too little!" Erin said. "If they'd been born last winter, maybe they could have grown big enough. They can't even take on the *myst* in the forest yet."

Joey considered the problem for a bit. "Then we'll just have to grow one." He picked up the first hatchling that he'd fed, who had stayed close to him all night. "Come, George," he said. "Let's get you fattened up."

The dragon bleated like a baby goat but climbed up onto Joey's shoulder as he walked across the field.

Erin turned to Joey's dad. "What do we do with the rest?"

Joey's dad turned a critical eye to the field around them. The dragons were all about the size of puppies. About as threatening as well, swatting at each other, jumping straight into the air when startled, or playing keep-away with a stalk of grass, each grabbing an end and pulling.

"I have a few ideas," he said, narrowing his eyes at one of the dragons that was "playing possum," looking for all the world like it had turned back into a regular rock again. "Come on, let's go rouse the neighbors."

Erin trailed after him, unsure. Joey's other siblings and cousins were all now watching over the dragons, looking as dazed as Erin felt.

"How are they going to defeat the horde?" Erin couldn't help but ask. The dragons were still all so little!

"We have a swarm, now," Joey's dad told her. "All we need now is a plan."

Erin followed after him, wondering if the small god who'd carted her around before would suddenly pick her up again while leaving the rest of the town to die, because the dragons weren't going to be nearly enough to defeat the horde.

# Thirty-Two

George happily scrambled up the tree Master pointed him to. There were so many good things to eat there! Tasty bugs. Creeping vines. And *myst*, pure and clean and sliding down his throat like fresh spring water.

He didn't know how he knew about water, about rain that came from the skies and tickled his belly. That was in the Time Before.

Many things had happened in the Time Before. Many things that George didn't understand, like the hands that passed over him, pressed *into* him, forming him. Or the cool magic that came from *Her*, that had wakened him and his brothers and sisters.

There were many things that George did understand. That now was the time of the quickening, the growing. That Master wanted George to grow as quickly as he could.

There was a threat George had to face. Buried deep in Master was *worry* so strong it tainted the air. Layers of magic hid it, but George could see the truth.

So George ate everything he could. Belched bigger and bigger blue flames.

And waited for Master to finally understand how they must join.

Or else he'd just have to take matters into his own claws.

# Thirty-Three

Joey kept an eye on George as he climbed high in the tree, seeking the *myst* hanging from the topmost branches. How much time did they have? Was the horde already approaching? How would he know? The day at least was clear and sunny, the sky pale blue with clouds high and thin painted across it. Joey didn't need the heavy jacket and scarf he had—his blood could warm him easily enough.

He still kept them wrapped tightly around him. He didn't want to give up even these traces that marked him as human. Or at least somewhat human.

His emotions were so far away, now. He remembered having them. He remembered feeling disgust and sorrow, homesickness and love. The strongest emotion he had anymore was curiosity.

Could he work himself into a rage? Possibly. But why bother? What was the point? His own fires could burn more brightly.

The *myst* whispered in the trees. Joey heard it so clearly now. He could see why it drove men *wyrd*. It promised things to him. Ideas that he knew were alien to him suddenly formed, like setting fire to his family's farm, since he was no longer a part of it and they had already begun to reject him.

He blocked the *myst* as well as he could. It was just one more thing he would have to get used to.

Joey tried to concentrate on George instead. The little dragon wasn't so little anymore. He was easily the size of a large dog, rapidly growing to small-pony size. George easily took on larger patches of *myst*. It backed away as he approached.

A couple of times the *myst* had tried to hook George, sending tendrils around his paws, like sticky ropes.

George had flamed them away, then gulped up what remains he could. The vines that tore into human flesh had no effect on his blue scales except to slow him down until he snapped at them with his sharp jaws.

The wildcat they'd discovered resting in one of the trees hadn't stuck around to see if its fangs and claws were any match for George's.

George didn't match the painting of a dragon that had been over the fireplace, that Joey had grown up with. His forearms were much larger, while his wings remained small. He was a six-legged creature, not four.

Would George fly using magic? Instead of his wings? Or would his wings grow later?

George could no longer reach the topmost branches of the trees, where the *myst* had retreated. He'd grown too heavy. With a much deeper roar instead of the cackle he'd had as a baby, George backed down out of the tree, like a cat, until he could jump down. Then he walked over to Joey and looked up at him.

After a few more trees, George wouldn't have to look up. He'd be eye to eye with Joey. He squatted on his rear with his head up, his long tail swishing the ground, knocking into bushes and vines.

"Hi," Joey said.

George appeared to be looking at Joey expectantly, though it was difficult to read his reptilian eyes. They were as golden as a magician's, but not human, not in the least.

George's color hadn't really changed as he'd grown. He was darker blue on the top of his back, fading to a whitish blue-gray along his belly. Scales covered every part of him. He had five yellow talons on all four feet, like two sets of hands.

His wings were *myst*-colored, pale and flimsy. They'd never carry his weight.

"What do you need?" Joey asked, his curiosity rising again.

George tilted his head to one side, then held out a front leg to Joey.

Curious, Joey came closer, then closer still, until he was just a few inches from the dragon.

George sighed and leaned forward, closing the distance, until he pressed against Joey, his head falling over Joey's shoulder.

Instinctively, Joey wrapped his arms around George. The dragon was warm, much warmer than Joey expected. He smelled of the trees he'd been climbing, of the green vines he'd been eating, as well as fresh frost, clean and bracing.

George gave another sigh and grabbed onto Joey's forearms tightly, his claws digging in.

Was George afraid that Joey was going to run away? Why?

When something louder than the *myst* started speaking inside Joey's head, he understood.

Part of Joey struggled to get away. *No!* He was going to be even less human, now, with this other voice in his head. This *alien* voice that spoke with rocks and ate magic.

And not just George. No. There were the others. All the other dragons. He could feel all of them, now.

All the alien thoughts drowning his own.

The voices became a whirlwind, sweeping him away. He danced on silver clouds with the dragons, under foreign skies, far from the earth. They mated and died for generation after generation, until their own sun started to die, their home world started to disintegrate.

The dragons plunged through the cold dark space between the stars, blown by their own exploding sun and propelled by the magic that lived in the dark places of the universe, those spots that Man had never found.

The earth welcomed them, the soft spaces underground, where they slept for thousands of years before being raised to the surface, knowing wind and rain and man's hand.

Until it was finally time to wake.

Joey wept as no magician had ever wept, overwhelmed by all the other voices in his head. Their loss, their great pilgrimage, their sacrifice, their determination to live again.

Finally, Joey came back to himself. They were no longer in the deep woods, but in a clearing.

George would no longer fit in the woods.

Joey looked up, and up, and up. George was easily as tall as the house Joey had grown up in.

George's forearms had not grown in proportion to the rest of him. They weren't useless, but they weren't his main defense.

His wings, though, were now magnificent. They shimmered, iridescent in the pale sunlight.

Joey instinctively knew the wind from those wings would blow a man over. Possibly a horse as well.

George was laughing at him. Why was Joey so surprised? George had become what Joey—what mankind—needed to fight the *myst*. That was the way of his kind. To become what was needed. Rocks to pass through the cold stars, dragons to live again.

The astonishment that filled Joey was also strange. He felt wonderment, and thankfulness, and awe.

*How?* Joey asked. He'd poked at his soul. He'd felt his emotion drain away.

*You didn't lose them,* George replied. *They were just buried. You seemed to miss them. I separated them. Or you would have lost them.*

Joey didn't quite understand how George had returned his emotions to him, while letting him keep his magic.

He still wasn't human, and never would be again. Not only was there magic in his soul, there were dragons. He'd never be alone with his thoughts. They'd always be there, haunting him, drawing him into flight with them.

It was possibly a cruel gift, letting Joey feel while still keeping him separate from the rest of humanity.

At the moment, Joey was grateful.

Joey reached out to the others. They weren't the size of George—none of them would reach his great height. But they'd grown as well. Some were still not much larger than a raven, while others were horse-sized and larger.

The chorus that greeted Joey felt alien and cool, like spring morning winds. He could feel them braiding their thoughts together so he wouldn't be overwhelmed again.

There were still so many. It felt to him like trying to drive a team of eight horses that weren't in step with each other. How could he manage them? He tried to imagine the reins in his hands, pulling them back.

It still felt like too much. It would take him time to learn.

Time he didn't have. Time none of them had.

George turned his head to the south. *They're coming.*

Joey felt them as well. The surge of *myst,* of its power. A rolling wall of hatred. Bearing down on Lakeland.

"Can we stop them?" Joey asked out loud, his voice sounding strangely alien to his own ears. More hoarse, as if he hadn't used it for ages.

*We can only try.*

With that, George leaned over, lying down on his belly. With a touch of magic in his step, Joey leapt up onto George's back.

"We'll need to do better than that," Joey murmured as he grabbed the reins again. There were no physical pieces of leather in his hands, but he felt them, nonetheless.

George gave a great *whuff* with his wings, jumping into the air, bending the trees back with the air he displaced.

Long trails of dragons flew behind them. Not the perfect V of birds, but regimented lines, like an army.

It was war.

# Thirty-Four

Carl/Jim generally sent the men forward in three waves.

The first wave would hit the barriers for the town, as usual. These were the most *wyrd* of the army, the ones who had lost the most of their soul and consciousness to the *myst*. They were the shock troops. The ones who didn't care if they lived or died. The ones that the *myst* wouldn't bother to cure if they were too injured.

The second group were the distance fighters, the ones with bows. They stood back and peppered the opposition. Sometimes they never moved out of their position.

The third group were the smarter fighters. They knew enough of towns to follow a street and chase men down. They also knew enough to recognize a trap when they saw it.

Today, though, outside of Lakeland, Carl hesitated. There was something different here. The barrier the town had set up across the gate looked as sturdy as all the others. He was certain archers and other distance fighters were set up just behind the gate, and would give his men a pretty fight.

It wouldn't matter in the end. Carl and his troop would win, drive into the town, burn what they could, maybe rest a day, and push on.

But still Carl hesitated to commit any group other than the shock troops. His scouts couldn't see any kind of traps set up in the road—like the one town that had dug pits full of stakes that had impaled the first set of fighters.

Even the *myst* seemed cautious here. Something was different. Carl could feel it in the air. The sun was bright in a pale blue sky, winter already setting in. Hearth fires burned and the comforting smell of smoke wafted over Carl.

Maybe there were more magicians here, like there had been at that other town. Magicians who had worked together to burn the *myst* away, weakening Carl and the army.

That must have been it. But Carl knew how to handle more magicians, now—just send more men that way, overwhelm them, then kill them.

Ima stood next to Carl, urging him to commit more troops. Not in words, no. But he felt her derision. *She* wouldn't be afraid to lose a few more men. It wasn't as if they couldn't turn half this town, replenish their men without much work.

Carl was still determined to be cautious. He sent forward only half of the shock troops. It was still a mass of roaring men, leaping out of the woods and ramming the gates. They screamed and howled, really quite frightening.

The town fought back, as he'd suspected, with distance weapons—arrows, darts, javelins, and rocks.

Rocks?

The rocks were brown-gray, dull on the outside. They looked ordinary.

Even from many yards away, Carl could tell they weren't.

*Don't touch the rocks!* he commanded all his men.

Too late.

One of the men—Emerson, if Carl remembered correctly—reached down and grabbed one of the rocks, probably one that had hit him. He hefted it, as if he intended to toss it back over the gate at the townspeople.

The rock transformed into a nasty blue lizard.

Startled, Emerson tried to pitch the lizard away. It leaped out of his hand and bit him, right on the nose, hanging from it like a long piece of snot.

Howling, Emerson whirled, swinging his head wildly, trying to get the lizard to let go.

Carl lost sight of Emerson as he danced away.

A surge of hate boiled through the men. They turned, as one, to where Emerson had gone.

Carl got a brief glimpse of Emerson as he looked around, his skin pale, his brown eyes looking lost. He reached out to the man, trying to draw him back into the fold.

Emerson stayed as he was.

His brothers on either side of him reached out to touch him, to grasp his shoulders, to fill him with *myst* again.

But Emerson still stubbornly stayed as he was, fully human with scared brown eyes.

How the hell had that lizard sucked the *myst* right out of him? Had it stolen all of the man's magic as well?

The men around Emerson roughly shook him. He gazed around wildly, looking lost. He screamed, the sound shocking in the nearly silent horde.

Why couldn't he be converted again? Why wouldn't he turn *wyrd*?

It must be an anomaly. Emerson had joined them in the last town. He must have been very different to start with.

Carl nodded.

The other men killed him, slicing his throat and letting him fall.

Then another got bitten by a lizard.

And lost his connection to the brothers around him.

Then another was turned. And another.

The men surrounding the ones who had been bitten wouldn't wait until Carl's order. The enemy was suddenly among them. They were killing their brothers.

Carl tried to refocus his troops. So what if a few men turned away from them? They must stay focused on the enemy: the town and the townspeople. The men must swarm the gate. Ignore the few who had suddenly turned traitor in their midst.

Then the man next to him shivered and shrank and turned human, his brother no more.

Had he been bitten by a hidden lizard? Or was there some unknown magic in force?

Jim killed the man with a quick twist of the head, snapping his neck.

*Retreat!* Carl called. The men had to retreat. Or he'd lose them, not to the townspeople or lucky hits, but to the other men who would tear them apart.

*RETREAT!* he called again.

The men didn't want to turn. The town was right there! There were people on the other side, people to burn, people to kill and tear to pieces.

But Carl had no defenses against rock lizards who sucked all the *myst* out of his men. And he'd lose most, if not all, of his shock troops if he didn't pull back.

*RETREAT NOW!* Carl called.

The men pulled back from the gate without turning around. Carl had learned that faceless men were easier to kill, even for the *wyrd*, so they never showed their backs when they retreated.

Before the men could pull back more than a few feet, the back of the army suddenly cried out. Men started running past Carl, going toward the town, away from something way back there.

Carl tried to sort through the impressions the men had. It was fire. And pain.

Finally, he grabbed one of the men who was running past, forcing him to stop and look at Carl, tell him what he'd seen.

*Dragons.*

# Thirty-Five

I ma could *not* believe what she was seeing. Huge, scaly, winged *dragons*. Dark blue, like an angry stream, with *myst*-colored wings and golden eyes that should have marked them as allies but instead, made them enemies.

Where the *hell* did they come from? The woods protected the horde, but they were too many to all fit along the trail. Some were caught out in a meadow. She stayed under the protection of the trees, watching the battle.

It was always best to know your enemy.

The monsters weren't all huge. Some were merely the size of dogs, about three feet through the body, with about that much tail as well added to the end. There were others, though, horse-sized and beyond. Not including the tail.

They weren't attacking, either. They just dipped down, diving like a hawk might at a pond, their snouts extended. They strafed the horde who raced through the open area, then flew back up, out of range.

What were they doing? It took Ima a while to figure out.

The *myst* that always floated above the horde: The dragons drank it down. Weakening the horde. Stealing the magic.

Ima fumed. *How dare they?*

The archers' arrows bounced off the tough scales of the dragons as they approached. However, the archers' aim remained true. One got a lucky shot, direct to the eye of one of the beasts. It screamed as it spiraled down, great clouds of *myst* and smoke billowing from it as it died.

That got the attention of the other dragons. They roared and belched flames at the remaining men.

The dragons had *fire* inside of them.

Ima could work with that.

She reached up, searching for the *spark* that lived inside the creatures. She focused on one that was the size of a small pony.

However, its alien coolness belied her fire. She couldn't find the focal point.

Maybe it was too small.

Ima searched again, going for a bigger creature. Inside that swirling mess of winter starlight and frost she found a flame that burned brightly. It was blue, the color of shadows, but hotter than anything she'd ever know.

It didn't take much for Ima to make that fire flare suddenly, burning through the fragile flesh that contained it.

The dragon exploded in mid-air, flaming all the way down to the earth, landing with a satisfying *thud*.

The attention of the *myst* suddenly focused on Ima. She could barely catch the words, however. It had lost so much of itself, had grown so much weaker.

*You can do that?*

*I AM the one*, Ima said firmly. Carl was nothing compared to her. The *myst* had chosen the wrong champion when it chose him.

*Go. Do my bidding.*

A flood of power surged in Ima. She felt herself light up. Her entire body became encased in flame.

Floating three feet above the ground, Ima left the shelter of the trees to do battle with the dragons.

# Thirty-Six

Beagle Boy watched the battle, hidden in a pocket of *nowhere*. He couldn't help the dragons. He could only hold back the *myst*. The webs he spun with his eight legs weren't strong enough to stop the fall of one of the great beasts. He couldn't put out the fires that erupted inside of them.

He threw back his head and howled in mourning with the passing of each great beast. They had so much knowledge to share! So much was being lost!

But how to stop the girl? She flared as bright as the sun in the center of the meadow, calling the dragons to her, just to watch them die.

Beagle Boy had never harmed a human before. They were his charge. He protected them. He couldn't kill one. Even one as infected with *myst* as the girl.

Could he save her, somehow? Drain the *myst* from her?

No. She'd lived too long on *myst* and magic. By this point, she would have forgotten how to eat. She'd never be able to go back to being human.

Could he take her the other way?

She would be an angry god. Vengeful. Like Angel and some of the other small gods, she wouldn't be tied to a territory. She would go to where she was needed.

And she would help people. As long as she was worshiped with flames and asked by people to enact their fury. Fury that wasn't right for them, but was right for a small god.

Another great dragon died.

Beagle Boy focused his attention on the girl. He started feeding her more power. Fanning her flames. Making her glow so brightly that even he could barely see her anymore.

Finally, she turned away from the dragons and looked to him.

*Why?* He was making her stronger. She could kill more beasts now.

Beagle Boy shared his vision of her. A goddess of fire. The Flaming One, perhaps. If she would take just one more step toward him.

People would venerate and fear her. Call on her to enact their vengeance.

She could burn for eternity.

*I would be The One?* she asked.

Beagle Boy wasn't exactly sure what she meant by that. *There is not another god of punishment or retribution.* The small gods protected people and the land. The world had been too deadly for man to focus on anything other than survival.

If the *myst* passed, The Flaming One might be called on often.

*Then I will join you,* the girl said.

She took one step across the meadow, then another, gaining altitude with each step. Fires blossomed at her feet.

Then she reached the level of the Beagle Boy, his pocket of *nowhere.* He held out one of his many hands, helping her take the next step, where *power* and *duty* and *connection* were all one.

And Ima passed from the consciousness of the world.

The legend of The Flamed One was suddenly born, the idea planted in the consciousness of man around the world. How she'd been born out of pain. What were the consequences of calling her. The details of the vengeance she would unleash.

How and when to call her, when need was great.

# Thirty-Seven

Carl stood just outside the cursed town of Lakeland and tried frantically to keep his troops alive. He directed men to scatter, under the trees, where they would be safer from the aerial attack.

But the smaller dragons hid in the brambles or were disguised as rocks along the path. Carl felt sections of his army unlink from his mind.

Too many had lost the *wyrd* and turned human again.

The horde was supposed to live forever! To cleanse the earth of man! Why didn't the dragons understand that? Why were they attacking the *myst*?

Carl hated them, these flying monsters. They confused him as well. The *myst* had never seen such creatures or encountered such flame. His thoughts slowed as the *myst* diminished.

There were many small gods, thousands all over the world. Never had the *myst* encountered such a strong enemy.

When Ima started fighting the dragons and winning, more power drained away from Carl. *No!* he shouted.

The *myst* ignored him.

Why couldn't it understand that dividing its attention that way was the surest path to failure? Carl raced down the road, heedless of the men he shoved out of the way, going to the field where Ima battled.

The intense light made Carl shade his eyes. He couldn't bear to look directly at Ima. She glowed with all the power of the *myst*. Dragons exploded in the air above her. They wheeled around, belching flame at her.

Ima just laughed and blew up another one.

She had always loved to set fire to things.

When Ima grew brighter still, Carl had to turn away. He couldn't see her anymore, just a glowing light, brighter than any sun.

He had the sense she was rising, each step in the air bursting into flames. Then she was gone.

Where did she go to? How had the enemy tricked her? She was too smart to fall for their lies, wasn't she?

The power of the *myst* slammed back into Carl as it focused on him again. But what could he do? He couldn't blow up the dragons like Ima. The horde was scattering. Troops of men still stayed together with their brothers—always stronger together—but the groups weren't connected any longer.

*Survive,* the *myst* hissed at Carl.

It needed for him to live through the battle. Regroup. Retrain. Come back and attack another day. Return with a stronger horde.

Suddenly, Carl had a vision of The Mountain in His glory. How it had calmed him, soothed him, to view The Mountain and witness His changes.

*No!* Jim screamed. *Burn. Claw. Attack. Until they're all dead.*

*But The Mountain,* Carl said. It was where they'd first gained strength. It was home.

They could go back to what remained of New Mountain Town.

The Mountain wouldn't permit dragons, Carl was certain of it. They could bide their time in its shadow. The *myst* would make them a haven, there.

So they could come back stronger.

Carl sent his men the image of The Mountain, what had drawn them all together in the first place. That clear view.

The two dozen men gathered around Carl growled their approval. These were the smartest of the horde, the least lost to the *wyrd*. They understood what he asked, and approved.

With *myst*-powered leaps, the men raced away, abandoning all the others, the ones too weak to follow, the ones already turning human, the ones too lost, who walked willingly into the flames.

Carl and his brothers would hide close to The Mountain, where none other dared come.

Until it was time.

Little Carl mourned as he ran, his body fueled by *myst*. There would be no more apples or soft bread. No more plans of bridges, no more hope of gentle spring.

The *myst* would fight on, but at its own time and choosing.

# Thirty-Eight

George saw the men racing away. He sent his flames dancing over them, burning away the *myst* that powered them.

They continued at speed, though a few fell away.

George rose up, flying ahead of them, then turned back. There was a field up ahead. The men could be stopped there.

He felt curiosity from Joey. The boy was so young. Though George had only been alive for such a short while, he felt as though he'd lived several lifetimes.

All his brothers and sisters, all their fighting and their pain had passed through him. All that knowledge lost. All the worlds they could have saved.

He only shared a sliver of that with Joey. The boy was still too easily overwhelmed.

He'd learn. Mankind would learn.

George shared with Joey the impression he had, of the *myst*-shaped man down there.

He was the leader. The one they had to stop. Or the *myst* would just keep coming back, growing stronger and attacking again.

Joey gave his consent, though George didn't really need it. He was, after all, the one flying.

*Can they talk?* Joey asked.

George thought about it, puzzled. Why would Joey want to talk with the men? Was it because he was still a man? Had it been a mistake for George to unbury Joey's emotions?

Perhaps.

But now George was curious. The *myst* had found its champion. What would it say?

He wanted to find out as well.

George settled on the far side of the closest meadow that the racing men were sure to cross. The Flaming One had already ascended. She would remain, though, and challenge the dragons now and again.

She wouldn't destroy any more of his brothers and sisters. Not unless her vengeance called for it. Her rule would be exact. Precise. As well as just, something she probably hadn't considered yet.

She would protect humanity in her own way, different than the rest of the gods.

George approved.

He'd barely settled when the first racing man leaped into the clearing. He still had the eyes of the *wyrd* though the magic was fading in him.

The others piled up behind him when he stopped.

Joey dismounted and went to stand in front of George.

A very tall man walked out from the rest.

This was the *myst*'s champion. His hair was gray and curly, almost as if it had been touched by the *myst*. His eyes glowed more like a magician's. There was something wrong with his face, his jaw shoved to one side, as if the world hadn't wanted to see his face and had turned it away.

And he could speak. Interesting.

# Thirty-Nine

Joey understood what George had meant when he saw the tall man move out of the rest of his group. He was the champion of the *myst*. It infused him, had touched his silver hair, was held in his golden eyes. He was misshapen, as all things the *myst* touched were, his jaw hinged wrong.

But he didn't wear anything that commanded attention, just a brown, homespun shirt with plain trousers and boots. No hat. No sash. No pins, like what Joey thought the ancient commanders had worn.

"Let us go," the champion commanded as he approached Joey.

"Why?" Joey asked reasonably enough. "You've killed thousands. Maybe millions."

"What do you mean?" the man asked, head tilted to the side. "The horde hasn't."

"The *myst* has," Joey explained.

"I am not the *myst*," the man said. "I am Carl."

Joey heard other echoes in that name, other names that the man had. But he'd take what he'd been given. "Joey," he said, introducing himself. "And I can't let you go."

"Then you'll have to kill me. Kill us," Carl said, indicating the men behind him.

Joey had killed Max, but only in self-defense. How could he kill an unarmed man who just stood there, peacefully?

They stood at an impasse.

Carl smirked. "Well, if you can't bring yourself to kill us, we'll just be on our way."

"I can't let you pass," Joey said quietly. He couldn't allow the *myst* to gather strength and return.

"So we're just going to stand here all day?" Carl asked. "I'm not sure your friend there would approve."

Joey didn't have to turn to George to know the dragon was already growing impatient. "I could just turn you over to him," Joey stated. "He would have no problem eating you up."

Carl's gaze turned hard. "He's an abomination, you know. Something not from this world."

"And the *myst* is?" Joey challenged.

Carl laughed. "It's in all of you. Everyone has magic. Everyone can touch the *myst*. You're the only one who can talk to those monsters."

Joey knew it was true. Though George had given Joey his emotions back, that didn't make him human. He could use that as well.

"Then maybe it's the time of monsters," Joey said quietly. He knew that Carl would never attack. Would stand there for days, feeding off *myst* and magic. Unmoving while vines grew up around his legs.

Until Joey turned away. Then Carl would continue on his path.

So Joey called on the blue fire waiting under his skin.

And attacked.

The blue flames lit up Carl, burning his clothes but not his skin.

Carl was mostly made of *myst* at that point. He could resist Joey's flames.

Joey burned hotter, calling on the rage that still lived in his blood. The anger from the deaths of all the dragons. How much he'd lost, and was sure to lose. How he'd be cut off from the rest of humanity, whether he had emotions or not.

Carl still laughed. He took another step forward, burning brightly, and flung his cold *myst* at Joey.

The attack struck Joey, sinking into him like a knife. The cold filled his heart. His emotions drained away again. He shivered and drew up his flames, but they failed to warm him.

All his magic was frozen by the *myst* and breaking off in pieces. Soon he'd be normal.

*Human.*

It was what the *myst* promised him. A normal life. He could marry Erin. Have children. Live on the farm with his family.

The *myst* could do that. Just as it could fill a man with magic, it, and only it, could take it away. Remove itself completely from Joey.

Let him live a normal life.

It would even break the link between him and the dragons. It would be only him in his head.

The blue flames tried to surge up, tried to warn Joey of the things the *myst* didn't mention.

He'd die with no affinity to magic. Even if he was watched carefully, sooner or later, the *myst* or one of its creatures would take him.

And if he cut his ties with the dragons, George would die.

Not right away, but George needed Joey's humanity as well, his connection to the earth, in order to live here.

Joey nurtured the vision the *myst* gave him, of a normal life, of Erin and kids and living out the changing seasons on his land. Indulged himself. Just for a little while.

Then he drew back. Looked at his children's lives. How they'd always live afraid of the *myst* and everything that went bump in the night. The howls and screams carried on the wind. Never able to run free in the fields but always on the lookout for birds or other beasts.

Joey treasured his humanity. Cherished it.

But he wanted more for all of mankind.

Joey called on the flames that lived in the deepest part of his soul. Flames that would burn the *myst*.

He erupted with fire, the flames shooting twenty feet in the air, before he directed them at Carl.

Dragon flames.

Carl screamed in agony, but he stayed in place. Why didn't he run away like his men? Was George holding him there?

Or was there something inside Carl that didn't want to get away? Something that all the *wyrd* had, that made them kill themselves eventually?

The stench from the burning body was much worse than it had been with Max, as though a rotting sea had just been belched up in the meadow. *Myst* poured from Carl's body, straight up to a hovering George, who gulped it all down.

"No!" Carl screamed, his face melting away. "I want to see The Mountain again!"

His screams wrenched at Joey, but he didn't allow his flames to die down.

The men behind Carl stood motionless, unable to help? Unwilling?

With a final, haunting scream, Carl dissolved into a pile of white ash which rapidly spread over the meadow, killing everything it touched.

This piece of land would be haunted forever, Joey knew.

The men at the edge of the woods finally moved. Some started toward Joey, blinking their eyes clear as the *myst* released its hold on them.

Most ran away, the *wyrd* having too tight a grasp on their souls.

Joey and the dragons would hunt them down someday.

And kill them all as well.

At the end of the day, Joey and George landed in the market square. Many of the dragons had already returned and were resting in the nearby fields.

It was a good thing that it was winter. No matter how the dragons had saved them, the townspeople would be angry if it was spring and they were destroying crops.

What were they going to do with so many dragons, anyway? There were still hundreds of them, in all different sizes.

Though Joey had to admit with pride that George was still the biggest by far.

Tom the mayor came up to Joey. His clothes were stained with soot, as was his face. Joey learned later that some of the *wyrd* men had made it through the gate and started setting everything they could on fire.

"Thank you," Tom said. "You and your dragons have saved Lakeland."

Joey opened his mouth, then closed it again. It hadn't been the town that he'd been trying to save.

"We shall have a feast!" Tom proclaimed. The people gave a ragged cheer. They were tired as well, had fought all day.

And evening would be coming soon.

Or could they gather at night, now? There was so little *myst* remaining. And what little strands that showed up were quickly gobbled by the dragons.

It would take time for people to trust the dark. Joey wasn't about to suggest it yet.

But things would change, as they always did.

"But what about the dragons?" came a young voice from the crowd. Joey recognized it as Nathan, his cousin. "Will they come and eat too?"

"No," Joey said, kneeling down so he could look at Nathan in the eye. "They eat *myst*. And that's all."

"What happens when all the *myst* is gone?" Nathan asked reasonably.

Joey stood up. He didn't know.

He looked at the field behind him, littered with dragon bodies.

What were they going to do with all these dragons?

Erin came walking up. "I know."

Joey hadn't asked the question out loud, had he?

"The Blue Dragon farm is the home of the dragons," Erin said, speaking loudly. "They won't leave on their own. We will have to lead them."

"Where?" Joey asked.

"To every town along the coast. Then inland. Lead them and leave the ones that find homes along the way." Erin's eyes gleamed as she spoke. "It will be the greatest migration ever seen. They'll seek out pockets of *myst*. Will stay in places that have good feeding."

"And what happens when there are more dragons born? Baby dragons?" Tom asked, looking worried.

"That won't happen." Joey was surprised to find himself talking until he realized it wasn't him doing the speaking.

George was speaking through him.

"Though we are sexed, male and female, we cannot procreate. After we are gone, there shall be no others."

While Joey knew that people in the town were relieved, all he felt was sorrow.

He hoped that dragons lived for a very, very long time.

"And if we go on this migration," Joey said, holding out his hand to Erin, "you might find your home."

Erin took Joey's hand. "I might." Then she leaned closer and kissed him on the cheek. "But I don't have to stay."

Joey gave Erin a hard look. "You understand what…what I am? What I'm not?"

Erin gave him a serious look. "I will stay with you. If you will have me."

Joey felt himself blush all the way to the tips of his ears.

Maybe he didn't have to give up all of his dreams after all.

# *Forty*

Inside the base of the tower, where what used to be the Schuller's folly had once stood, sat a rock.

It wasn't like the others. It was red, the color of dried blood. Instead of being oval, it was roughly square. And it felt...familiar.

Since it was buried by the debris from the hatchlings, none of the humans noticed how it started to glow when the evening frost first touched it.

The rock sang softly to itself of the coming spring and gentle rains sure to follow for her and her sisters. How the summer sun would quicken the spirit laying deep within, and the brightly colored leaves would engage her heart.

How when winter came again, she and her sisters would have absorbed enough of tendrils of magic to rise again.

# About the Author

Leah Cutter writes page-turning fiction in exotic locations, such as New Orleans, ancient China, the Oregon coast, rural Kentucky, Seattle, Minneapolis, Budapest, and other places.

Her short fiction includes literary, fantasy, mystery, science fiction, and horror, and has been published in magazines, anthologies, and on the web.

Read more stories by Leah Cutter at www.KnottedRoadPress.com.

Follow her blog at www.LeahCutter.com.

# About Book View Café

**Book View Café** is a professional authors' cooperative offering DRM-free ebooks in multiple formats to readers around the world. With authors in a variety of genres including mystery, romance, fantasy, and science fiction, Book View Café has something for everyone.

**Book View Café** is good for readers because you can enjoy high-quality DRM-free ebooks from your favorite authors at a reasonable price.

**Book View Café** is good for writers because 95% of the profit goes directly to the book's author.

**Book View Café** authors include Nebula, Hugo, and Philip K. Dick Award winners, Nebula, Hugo, World Fantasy, and Rita Award nominees, and *New York Times* bestsellers and notable book authors.

www.bookviewcafe.com